Now I Am Here

Chidi Ebere

Now I Am Here

PICADOR

First published 2023 by Picador

This edition published by Picador 2024
an imprint of Pan Macmillan
The Smithson, 6 Briset Street, London EC1M 5NR
EU representative: Macmillan Publishers Ireland Ltd, 1st Floor,
The Liffey Trust Centre, 117–126 Sheriff Street Upper,
Dublin 1, D01 YC43
Associated companies throughout the world
www.panmacmillan.com

ISBN 978-1-0350-0403-4

The epigraph is from Hannah Arendt, *The Life of the Mind*
(London: Secker and Warburg, 1978).

1 3 5 7 9 8 6 4 2

A CIP catalogue record for this book is available from the British Library.

Printed and bound by CPI Group (UK) Ltd, Croydon, CR0 4YY

Visit **www.picador.com** to read more about all our books
and to buy them. You will also find features, author interviews and
news of any author events, and you can sign up for e-newsletters
so that you're always first to hear about our new releases.

My heartfelt thanks to Ingrid, a constant source of inspiration and strength; to Eleanor, who believed in me, and for her calming guidance; to Ansa, for saying yes, and smoothing out the narrative wrinkles; to the exceptional team at Picador who took a chance and gave this work a welcome abode; and to you, the reader, for honouring these pages with your attention.

The sad truth is that most evil is done by people who never make up their minds to be good or evil.

Hannah Arendt, *The Life of the Mind*

1

My love, it is finished and we are done. Here is a sad truth: your eyes will never read these words, though each one is addressed to you. At least your mind shall have no need to worry about the truths contained herein. Three days ago, we received a message: 'Due to adverse conditions and events on the ground, planned reinforcement and/or resupply cancelled.' Today, our once great army lies in tatters, scattered across the fields and forests of the East. The enemy we thought vanquished, whose bones we trampled over, has performed a certain magic and risen from the dead. The Easterners have put an end to our forward march and tear through us as if we are sheets of cheap paper. It turns out that we, the invincible forces of the NDM, are not supermen, but ordinary beings of flesh, blood and bone.

You knew this would be our ruin. You warned me. I did not listen, and now the end rushes towards us at increasing speed. Moments are now so precious. This understanding has freed me from a prison of sorts. I was locked into a state of mind. An acceptable 'lodging' within which I hid my feelings and conscience. Such an arrangement allowed me to travel through this war: carrying out my duties to the letter, fully committed, always deeply involved. Such a hiding place is of no use under current circumstances. There is also a new, last-minute clarity. From this position I see <u>how</u> (though do not understand <u>why</u>) the collective madness we welcomed as a nation of blind souls led us into an abyss. At the moment of writing, I have no idea about the news and mood back home. Has the truth arrived? Have you woken from the dream and entered the nightmare? Give it time. Those of us in receipt of our just rewards watch as this episode approaches its finale. We are falling, and there is nothing to slow our descent. Many of us tremble and worry on the inside, though not in panic. We understand and accept these circumstances. Our apprehension exists because we have seen and know what ugliness comes your way. Reports trickle in from those fortunate enough to escape the approaching beast: the Easterners feast on blood and see no need for prisoners.

*

Hunger for vengeance, which the Easterners have in abundance, is a potent fuel for any killing machine. The Eastern enemy behaves as nothing we have seen before. I tell you, at our absolute worst, during our darkest moments, we never slaughtered in this manner. When circumstances necessitated our taking of life, there was always a reason, a logic to our actions. No matter how distorted our justifications, the existence of such reasoning gave us licence to function as we did. The enemy we face today is worse than a barbarian and wilder than any animal I know: they kill without hesitation. They kill with joy, and kill without rules.

We spent yesterday morning and most of the afternoon fleeing from these wild hordes. Placing as much space between our backs and their claws as possible, we retreated west, towards home, until a wall of Eastern armour said 'No further!' and sent the survivors scurrying back to our current position. Then, at 1723, the fighting stopped. Bullets remained in their magazines. Shells let us be. The enemy found other things to do. A silence fell over our part of the world. No wind, no birds. The groans of our wounded faded. A strangely comforting fear sang along every nerve in my body. My eyes noticed colours I had never seen before. I could read the clouds up ahead as if they were tomorrow's papers: column after column announcing our defeat. Glory was not ours.

The remnants of our battalion gathered together and made the necessary preparations. The arrangement of defences was completed without fuss. We ignored the futility of our actions. We are the mice, the enemy a vindictive cat playing a waiting game. The moment boredom sets in, it will crush us. No matter how great our bravery, honour and determination, there is no defence against what we face. Setting aside the fact that we are outnumbered by a truly hopeless ratio, we also have a finite supply of ammunition. How many more assaults can our bullets repel?

This camp at the forest's edge will be our resting ground, and we have no choice in the matter. Not in the <u>when</u>, and minimal influence in the <u>how</u>. This realization sent me into a thoughtful loop as I stared at all around me: a last opportunity to inspect the world. A jagged shadow. A card game. An automatic rifle at rest. Tent flaps conversing with the breeze. Two men engage in a chessboard battle, backs hunched forward, heads leaning in. A water can. An abandoned bandage, twisted and clotted with blood. Who owns those boots? A holy book calls out for a believer. Some find energy to talk and laugh. A few suppress curses and rue their misfortune. Here and there, solo characters read or focus on faraway points. The shapes and smells, the colours and other components of my immediate surroundings wait patiently to be registered by my senses, while there is still a chance.

These current circumstances bend our courage and test its strength. We camouflage all awareness of the fast-approaching conclusion. In this we almost succeed, but the truth is there to see in our eyes and general demeanour. At this moment, we thank heavens for our training. It helps us remember how to act as brave men should: we grit our teeth and pretend. Defeat and death are just 'things' that happen from time to time. It is an interesting form of theatre.

A new today. It is now 0809. The Easterners continue to bless us with an uncanny silence. We sense them out there, in between the shadows and foliage. Waiting, watching, invisible. Our eagle-eyed lookouts stare at the camp perimeters and beyond, yet remain blind. This is our enemy's land. They know it, and we do not. We wait in our holding position, surrounded on every side by bloody retribution. The waiting makes us anxious: it gives us too much time to think.

In order to burn off nervous energy, I begin an inventory of personal belongings. Among the items to be catalogued is this journal. A gift from another life. The cover has taken a light bruising (it has lived at the bottom of my bag all this while), but the paper within remains clean and uncreased. I stare at it and remember.

You were sad, frightened, and constantly fussed at invisible flecks of lint on my uniform. You cried, and apologized for your tears. 'Tears keep you human,' I said. You tried to laugh. You managed a smile, and then handed me a blue paper package tied with string. I fumbled with the knot. Your fingers, cool and dry and strong, took hold of mine and guided them through the unwrapping process. You whispered, 'Fill these pages with your adventures!' You mentioned the journal again, a quiet reminder, at the end of my last visit home. A solemn affair. Seasonal winds moaned and spread dust along the station platform. You asked why the faces of soldiers boarding the train were either sad, tired or terrified. There was no need to solicit your thoughts on my face. We had spent most of my leave wrestling with the matter of our business in the East. You asked what had I done to change as I had. I said nothing. You asked whether the rumours, reported in the foreign media, about NDM behaviour in the East were true. I replied with a grumble about the need to keep work and family life separate. 'And what happens when work changes the family member?' you asked. I remained silent.

Later. The stationmaster's whistle. Those left behind sobbed, and tears filled the eyes of all departing. From you, a final expression of understanding: 'I know it is hard for you to talk. I do.' You said, 'Write down your thoughts. It will help.' The train began its journey east. You followed, blowing kisses. You ran, yet the space between us grew.

I had completely forgotten about the journal. For a while, I wonder how it could help me. An hour later, conversation with fellow soldiers and private thoughts about the East have pushed the journal out of mind. The truth is, until now, I have been too busy adventuring and fighting for Our Dear Leader and the Greater Glory to write. There was only enough time to scratch down a date on the first page. The date is two and a half years old.

Perhaps the sudden appearance of the journal, at this late stage, is no coincidence. It calls out for my attention.

I hear its voice. Or is that simply the imagination running scared? Our situation has infected my thinking with mild superstition. By the way, these are not the words of a man attempting to make last-minute contact with a supreme being. There is no need to converse with any God who saw this bloody business and refused to intervene. The journal's reappearance also coincides with my new-found conviction (but a few hours old) that there is a correct manner for me to step away from the living: stripped naked by the truth.

Last night I had a dream. The first in many months. In the middle of a twitchy sleep, my mind transformed into a private cinema. 'Now Showing: Re-runs of Recent History!' Endless reels of full-colour action, starring me. The content was grim and shameful. These were not films I cared to see. Yet, no matter how I struggled and twisted, it was impossible to avert my eyes or turn my head. I could not leave my viewing position in order to switch off the projector. Within the dream I believed an external force (with a mighty grudge) held me captive, brainwashing me with mad images. Common sense returned the moment my eyes jumped open, and saw the films for what they were: honest recordings of my own deeds, shot from a frighteningly revealing perspective. Perhaps circumstances have chased these terrible memories from their hiding places. As an aggressive cleansing caustic, they eat away at my nerves.

It would be impossible to live and function well in civilian society with what I carry inside. Time is short and these vivid recollections make me restless. Like the air in a distended balloon, the memories need to get out. A disquiet fills my heart, which has nothing to do with a fear of death. The worries about dying sooner than planned exist because of the cargo carried by my conscience: heavy, rotten and bitter. A by-product of my actions. Memories too ugly to travel with me to the other side.

Two hours ago, on the way back from a mission to empty my bladder, I experienced a sudden, violent rupture within my chest. A furious pain. I waited for a distant crack to confirm this was a sniper bullet's work. I heard nothing but the grind of my clenched teeth. I looked down, my breast was clean. Unscathed, unbloodied, yet the pain was such that I could barely stand, hardly breathe.

I leaned my back against a nearby tree. Panting. Trembling. I closed my eyes and watched a thousand shades of red and yellow burn a path across my mind. Like a bushfire, though much faster. Had I fallen into terminal madness? It was not a constant pain, rather a series of eruptions: here, then gone. Here, then gone. A pulse. For fragments of a second, and much confused, I wondered 'what?' and 'why?' and 'how?' Then it clicked. I understood. The source of pain was not external, the torment within came from my own heart. My heart, which I believed long since crumbled into dust, had returned! It announced its presence with a ravenous agony that chewed through my chest and consumed my soul. This may sound strange to you, but I suddenly filled with joy. Like a child who received every item on a list of birthday gifts, I became ecstatic. 'Everything all right, sir?' a passing soldier asked. I looked. I smiled and nodded. The reason for my happiness was the pain tearing through my system. The discomfort was proof I still had a beating heart. An important realization: it meant I was not yet one of the living dead. My heart: I feel it bleed. I hear it weep.

Sad cries. My heart remembers, and brings you here. My face against your neck. Warm. Just right. I breathed you in until it was impossible to know where one of us ended and the other began. Not once during this war had I imagined <u>never</u> seeing you again. Today, there is no longer any need to imagine. How I wish everything I see around me was a trick of the imagination, the unshakeable sense of doom an illusion.

We will never meet again. You will never hold me again. I will never touch you, never hear your laughter, or listen to you sing again. We will never quarrel over tiny matters, and then make everything good once more. We will never dance together again, or be drenched by a shower. No more sitting for coffee and cakes at our favourite corner café while commenting on the world passing by. There is not enough time to list all the busy-ness we will never get up to, and it hurts. For a moment, I am a child, wishing for some great and mysterious power to take pity and grant me a little more time with you . . .

There are other reasons for my weeping heart. All I am going to miss: the sounds, the tastes, smells, colours, the change of seasons. The sights, words, music and the food! Friends and family, those known only by sight. Hills, clouds, water, all of it. Such a shame. No more home for me. Multiples of unfinished conversations with cousins, aunts and uncles. Endless unanswered questions still float around my head. What am I supposed to do with them all?

In the meantime, as if our present circumstances are not sour enough, a question buzzes around my head: 'How did I get here?'

It is impossible to hold this journal and not think of you. 'It will help.' Yes, and I know you hear me. Perhaps not my words, but certainly you still feel my existence, out there. Listen. Then there is also the fact I know of no better listener, no one else with your strength and patience. And so, this is where we are: I, who never writes, have suddenly discovered the joy of penmanship. Your memory and this journal have saved me.

My plan is to retrace the final segment of my journey from <u>then</u> to <u>here</u>, and present the memories in a clear and logical fashion. Regarding the content: I have spent my time in the East wading through terror and blood. This has moulded my character into its present shape. All is twisted, especially my tongue. The funny-sweet radio transmissions that once tickled your ears are gone. Lost. As is my light. Today's words are heavy with blood, and death runs through them: such is the nature of my deeds. The acts I have committed will hurt and confuse you. They will challenge you to prove you knew nothing, saw <u>nothing</u> of this in me. I am sorry. Our elders say: 'Circumstances make the shrimp bend as it does.' Along the way, circumstances opened doors within me that had best been left shut. The pain you feel is the truth burning away your illusions. In time, it will fade.

2

We are here, and all is not well. It has been this way for some time. The first signs of difficulty appeared nine months ago when the Easterners discovered cracks and weaknesses in our war machine. Our onward march slowed to a crawl. We no longer captured territory with ease and speed. Every step forward came at a great price: materiel, blood and lives. Directives from NDM High Command, which had once been tethered to well-reasoned strategy, dissolved into nonsense. Only those well away from the slaughterhouse and detached from the truth of battle could think in this manner. However, our programming to carry out orders overrode our doubts. We employed the best of our skills and convinced the men to believe in fairy tales. For a while, our efforts paid off.

Six months ago, our air superiority evaporated. A mighty God (without doubt operating at the enemy's side) puffed her cheeks and blew the NDM Flying Forces out of the skies. The Easterners employed a new class of anti-aircraft weapon, lethal and agile. We could no longer move forward. We dug in and considered how to regain momentum. In the meantime, the Easterners, rather than attack our static army divisions, turned their attentions to our inadequately protected supply units, whose speciality was hauling and moving, <u>not</u> fighting. For every tonne of materiel that made it through, another seven were lost.

Attaining the Greater Glory had become a burdensome task. Our problem, the result of a self-inflicted wound: we lost focus. What purpose did our fighting, burning and terrorizing serve? We could no longer say. Our orders were to teach the Eastern natives the meaning of terror. This we did, until the Easterners decided enough was enough and turned events upside down. Our losses were such that national conscription was introduced. Back home, the NDM crowed: 'The nation calls on all able-bodied men to step forward as fighting heroes! Lead the nation on to victory and the Greater Glory!' Our ranks began to fill with average men chasing foolish dreams. They were swiftly consumed by the fighting. The 'below average' were then invited to enter the fray. The result was an acceleration of the appearance and disappearance of new faces. The quality of the recruits plunged until most of the soldiers joining the melee resembled children. Lost, frightened and teary-eyed. 'Where are we going?' 'What are we doing?' their faces ask. I suppress the urge to tell them to be calm, and accept their role as guinea pigs in an experiment to discover the depths to which a man can sink, if given the necessary clearance. The children do not need my cynical words.

Our enemy began to fight like people protecting their families, land, culture, stories . . . They abandoned fear. For two of the most brutal months I experienced in this war, we held our ground. We stood, we fought, we bled, we died, and watched as the Easterners, perhaps having inhaled the sweet perfume of blood and victory, developed an unquenchable thirst for slaughter. We pulled back westward. Metre after metre, fallen man after fallen man. Word from NDM High Command: under no circumstances should our rearward movement be viewed as a retreat. It was a 'necessary tactical adjustment'.

One especially beautiful evening, thirteen days ago, we learned the enemy had cut through our lines to the north. Three days later, the same happened to our south. Their aim was clear: encirclement. Wrap a giant noose around our army's neck and then choke us out of existence. We were ordered to increase the pace of our 'necessary tactical adjustments' to the west. We vacated territory by the kilometre. We abandoned everything that slowed us down: the munitionless heavier weapons, fuelless vehicles and the wounded. I am extremely proud of the men we left behind. Not one of them asked us to hasten their end. This would be an understandable choice, given the condition of many. Instead, all they requested were rifles, bullets and a few grenades. They were ready to do what was necessary.

A week ago, the fighting eased off. Sporadic sniper fire, that was all. A ceasefire. A chance to catch our breath while NDM High Command and the Eastern leadership began the process of discussing an end to the war. We received a new set of orders: hold position until further notice. Our response was to advise against. Local intelligence revealed the enemy had continued to close in from both north and south: our western exit narrowed by the hour. Were negotiations to fail and the fighting start up once more . . . our entrapment and defeat would be likely. We abandoned such thoughts. Of course that could never happen, once NDM High Command understood our true position. We requested permission to head twenty kilometres west, minimum, and regroup with the remains of other units in the area. Request denied. The peace negotiations were a game of bluff, and Our Dear Leader could not afford the appearance of weakness that further movement west would give. They reiterated our orders to hold position. Supplies and reinforcements were promised within twenty-four hours. The parts within us that wished to remain alive kicked up a fuss. We felt the noose tighten. Instinct screamed: 'Get out! Move now!' But our training prevailed: it suppressed common sense and knocked aside the truth. We obeyed. We waited.

It was a long twenty-four hours. Eventually we learned a 'technical matter' had delayed the reinforcement/resupply process for at least another day. Again, and this time with the greatest urgency, we made clear that our survival, in the event of a fresh outbreak of hostilities, depended on either immediate reinforcement, or moving our units west as swiftly as possible. NDM High Command thanked us for our input. They repeated their promise to fulfil all requests within a reasonable time frame. We also received a gentle 'reminder' that those with an overview of the situation saw what the rest of us could not. We resisted the temptation to scream and tell them they were too distant from the action to understand. Encirclement would mean defeat. NDM High Command claimed to know what they were doing, they asked us to have faith. We waited. Twenty-four hours came and went.

Three days ago our circumstances took a turn for the worse. At 0815 we received confirmation the enemy's encirclement was complete, our westward route home blocked. Later, at 0927, we learned ceasefire negotiations had ended without success. Hostilities would resume at noon. Unfortunately adverse conditions and events on the ground prevented the timely reinforcement and resupply of our units. NDM High Command praised everything we had done for the Greater Glory. They praised our courage and fighting spirit, said we were in the thoughts of 'every man, woman and child in the nation!' Finally, we were reminded of our duty to honour Our Dear Leader, the nation and our uniforms, by fighting to the last man. The communiqué's footnote encouraged us to take the opportunity provided by current circumstances and inspire the nation with the ferocity of our final stand. There has been no contact with NDM High Command since.

I spent a good half-hour thinking how best to share the news. As you can imagine, it was an unusual situation.

Usually our troops surrounded, outnumbered and out-gunned others. Not this time. The expectation (during moments such as these) was that I deliver a composition of words with the power to light a fire in the men's guts. A speech to gather their spirits and make from each and every one a raging warrior: willing and ready to battle to the very end with such ferocity, our demise would become the substance of legend. As it is, <u>expectation</u> and <u>reality</u> are not always the best of friends. How should I tell the men our last hope had been crushed beneath the heels of circumstance? Half of my spirit felt tired and empty. It begged to lie down, sleep and not wake again. The other half reminded me that these men were my brothers and my sons. We had travelled here as one, and as one we had eaten, drunk, fought, burned, smashed and killed. As one, you know . . . I apologized to the men for my shortcomings, for my inability to shepherd them away from these killing grounds, and for leading them to defeat.

It was a sad, drawn-out moment as I explained our situation: we were truly beyond help and hope. The men listened. Some glared out at the world with anger. Others stared at the grass below. Some looked at me with relief.

Others remained indifferent. Many were tired. Some were so disturbed by the thought of our end at the enemy's hands, they suggested self-inflicted head shots as an easier way out. For a few seconds, morale threatened to crumble. After all, it is only the mad who welcome death without a shiver or a tear.

I remembered a scene towards the end of a popular war film. It was almost over for a group of fighting men (their situation, like ours, was hopeless). One after the other, the soldiers walked up to their CO and told him what an honour it had been to fight at his side. They were humbled and proud to stand with him one final time. It was a beautiful scene. Around me, the approach of death did not generate such packaged drama. The camp atmosphere became a sad, weighty grey. We knew running was pointless: there was nowhere to go. What to say? I looked around and took inspiration from the men's faces. 'We are soldiers,' I said. 'We do not run. No matter the circumstances. No matter the horror. Regardless of whether victory is ours, or belongs to the enemy, we are soldiers. Let us use the time we have left to make peace with ourselves.' The men understood. Tired souls creaked as they pulled together the remains of their warrior spirits. I watched backs straighten. A beautiful spark of defiance and courage appeared once again in their eyes. I listened to the coughs and sighs as the men looked within and made ready. In that moment I felt a great love for every one of them.

3

I now remember the start of my journey to this place. That hot, magical afternoon as you and I sat on the banks of Little River. The sun was especially bright. The blue above made us dizzy, as we pointed out creatures and shapes in the clouds. The air, sweet and warm, filled us with love. That was a happy moment. I remember it and smile. Our need to be together had become an addiction, surviving longer than an hour without the other was insufferable agony.

Now, however, we sat in silence, on the edge of uncomfortable. A few minutes earlier, you had concluded a lecture on the need for a life plan that looked further than the here and now. 'What are you going to do with yourself?' you had asked. I knew what you meant, yet tried to deflect your query with humorous commentary on various professions, complete with theatrical impersonations. My actions were blown off course by your impatient sigh. I froze, somewhat ashamed at having the truth presented in this way. You knew I had no idea about any of my future tomorrows, and I had no idea how to cope with you seeing this in me. To lose you, not to another, but due to my own aimlessness, was a terrifying thought. It dried my throat and locked my tongue. Then, with a touch and a laugh, you took the moment's gravity and placed it to one side.

We stood. We walked, fingers intertwined, talking, laughing . . . every so often we stopped for a kiss. Then, as if sent by great and mysterious forces, two butterflies, orange and brown, appeared out of the bushes and began to dance about our heads! You claimed they were a butterfly couple happy to share the company of lovers. You suggested we had been butterflies in previous lives. Our new orange and brown friends recognized this, and tried to communicate in a language we had long since forgotten. I remember how our attempts at psychic communication with the butterflies ended in nothing but static and laughter. Perhaps we should have tried harder, as you suggested. In the end, we agreed their presence was an omen. A beautiful omen.

I think about that day now. I had been about to write on another matter, when a sudden commotion interrupted my thoughts. Raised voices and <u>laughter</u>! The laughter was especially surprising, as I cannot remember the last time we heard such within our ranks. Laughter has become too afraid to visit our patch of earth.

I searched for the source of the fun, and saw a trio of men using shirts and other garments in a poorly coordinated attempt to guide something out through the main opening in the tent. My first thought was to believe the war had finally broken their minds. But mad they were not. They were simply happy to chase that 'something' around the tent. It took a few moments to discover the object of their attention. Into a slice of early morning sunlight flew a butterfly. Black with fluorescent blue dashes. It was beautiful.

Rather than leave through the available exit, the creature seemed to toy with its pursuers. The action was cyclical in nature: as the butterfly approached an opening lined with the glow of a sunny outside, the men's voices rose in an expectant cheer, reminiscent of the terrace crowds as the ball approaches the goal. The pitch of the voices reached a high-frequency peak, before collapsing into a groan of disappointment and more laughter. The butterfly had an independent streak. It performed a loop the loop that returned it to the middle of the tent, from where it continued its exploration. The message being, it would be with us a while longer. A brief pause, and then the pursuit began again.

The men made another five attempts to steer the creature towards the exit and, as always, at the last moment the butterfly changed its mind and headed to a location beyond the reach of the groaning, laughing soldiers. Such a wonderful sight. Simply and effectively, the butterfly transformed the grey mood inside the tent into one of joy. Perhaps that was its mission: provide a moment of light entertainment and distraction. A temporary respite from the gloom and weight of the inevitable.

Another (unsuccessful) attempt left the men gasping, perspiring and grinning. The butterfly made two more circuits of our space. These included trips around our heads, hops from one object to another, and a brief stop on this journal. Finally, perhaps because its work was done, the butterfly flew off on a dusty beam of sunlight. Its departure was met with a chorus of tender sighs. For a few moments we shared a collective joy at the butterfly's 'escape'. The idea that something we cared for could get away from this grim location filled us with light.

The men are presently involved in a noisy debate about the butterfly: was its presence an omen or not? An optimistic minority argue its appearance is a hopeful sign. 'Such beauty in these hopeless circumstances is no coincidence,' they say. 'When did we last notice an insect, let alone one as beautiful as that?' The practical majority swat these beliefs aside: 'We were too busy with war to notice Nature's minutiae. The butterfly is a butterfly, as simple as that.' I choose not to involve myself in the discussion. Instead, I marvel at how this war has shaped our minds. The butterfly's appearance becomes a key. A box of long-forgotten memories opens up. Here I sit, with nowhere to go but the end, and the thoughts in my mind are of happier days.

On that hot afternoon by the river, the butterflies escorted us to your front door (the better part of two kilometres away). Then, with you gone, I received their undivided attention on the walk home through Nation Park. Such was my preoccupation with the creatures, I failed to notice the private barbecue until my path was blocked by a large grill, filled with glowing embers and covered with sizzling, browning meat. The guests were young men of a similar age to myself. Their uniform dress (anthracite chinos, grey short-sleeved shirts, black belts, silver buckles, black ties, black sandals) was casual. They were not. These were NDM people!

You remember my view of the NDM at the time. By the late afternoon of this encounter, the National Defence Movement had ruled for three and a half years. The memories of their takeover are still clear. Endless hours of martial music on every radio station in the country. The telephone lines silent. Not even the hum of disconnection. I knew about military coups. Read news pieces about them taking place in faraway lands, listened to experts on the radio discuss such matters. But that did not prepare me for the thrill of one day finding myself in the middle of such a business. I dashed out into the city and began wandering around. Trucks, tanks, soldiers, blockades. The NDM troops went about their business without saying very much. Meanwhile, I was free to move around and look, though it was impossible to travel longer than five minutes without being stopped and asked to present papers. At 0943 two uniformed ladies approached me. They studied my documents for longer and with greater care than any of the other officials I had interacted with. I asked why the military were everywhere. Was this a coup d'état? Where were the heads of government? They ignored my queries, suggested I head home, listen to the eleven o'clock broadcast, and all would become clear.

The NDM wished to make a point. Their first 'grand' action was a public and brutal elimination of the previous government. At 1100, our new champion, the Dear Leader, addressed the nation from an unusual setting: a live radio broadcast on Nation Beach. The microphones picked up the squawks of seabirds passing comment in the background, and the faint sighs of the sea wind.

'Mothers, fathers, sisters and brothers . . .' The Dear Leader's voice was calm and warm. 'As a soldier, I took an oath to protect the health of our nation. As a soldier, I was taught to fend off external threats. As such, I never imagined the greatest threat to our well-being would come from within . . .' He then asked us to look around and see how the nation had been choked by incompetence, nepotism, daylight robbery and disdain for honest, hard work. A rotten gift from the previous leadership.

A first set of newspaper photographs showed twenty-nine members of the former government tied to stakes, arranged in a grid on Nation Beach. The sea appeared calm, as if it did not wish to stir up unnecessary trouble. The Dear Leader shared his vision of a way forward.

He gave us a clear path and attainable goals. He spoke of harnessing the nation's creative potential, of building greatness upon a foundation of dignity, honesty and transparency. I truly thought him mad at the time. What did he take us for, fools? We knew this song, had heard it a hundred times before.

His voice then changed in tone. We heard the fizz of suppressed rage, we heard disgust. The Dear Leader spat out a list of the former government's crimes and misdeeds. An eleven-minute-and-twenty-three-second inventory of criminal actions. The recital was followed by two minutes of quiet. We heard the gentle wind. The seabirds continued to deliver sporadic commentary, and we heard the sound of hard to distinguish metallic clicks and taps. We soon understood.

The Dear Leader picked up the executioner's cloak and wrapped it around his shoulders: twenty-nine shots, ten to fifteen seconds apart. Crack! A life gone. Crack! A life gone. It was terrible and sad. A second set of newspaper photographs showed the twenty-nine former members of our government: bloodied chests, heads bowed, bodies held upright by ropes. I remember sitting, frozen. I tried to leave my chair. I had to switch off the radio. My body refused to move. I sat and listened.

A majority of the nation's citizens applauded the Dear Leader's actions. I understood how years of political, social and economic abuse at the hands of the previous government could make one fed up enough to believe execution without trial was acceptable. At the same time, what was the point of having a National Law if we resolved such matters with bullets? By the way, I never managed to erase the memory of those twenty-nine gunshots.

Regardless of my horror at the public executions, I must admit the NDM were not the same familiar, arrogant, incompetent opportunists in a different guise. The Dear Leader and the NDM surprised us by keeping their promise to 'use our wealth and set us free'. The fortune generated by our considerable industrial capacities was channelled <u>back</u> into the nation. The sudden monetary abundance twisted the spirits and upset the mental balance of some who came to believe (encouraged by nefarious characters who watched from the sidelines) that wealth could be a salve for low self-esteem, or a filler for various spiritual cavities. The Dear Leader and the top echelons of the NDM stepped in when the infectious vulgarity that had entered our way of thinking threatened to become the norm.

Another, rarely discussed aspect to the NDM was the violence. Rumours. Whispers. Nothing overt. Within my circles and beyond, hushed voices spoke of someone who heard from somebody else who knew how the NDM dealt with those they did not like. 'Excessive!' 'Crossing the line!' 'Ugly!'

The NDM acts of violence were all grapevine stuff. My eyes had yet to witness any acts of brutality. But the rumours . . . If anything, their volume had increased in recent months. The whispers had built to a cacophony, and National Radio, the NDM mouthpiece, was forced to step in and dismiss claims of such incidents as fairy tales and fantastical gossip. They also informed us of the subversive and unpatriotic nature of these allegations. Rumours aside, I had no interest in experiencing 'fantastical gossip' first-hand. Yet, in spite of all the scheming and energy spent avoiding contact with NDM types, here I was.

At the barbecue, I looked around at the NDM officers. A voice within told me to be calm, to show no fear. I viewed matters of violence, fighting and the like as foolish, painful and unnecessary activities, at the time. That said, I never ran from a fight. Up until my late teens I was involved in a number of physical contests, in defence of one honour or another. Some fights were won and others lost. That afternoon, experience told me that if, as a result of my gatecrashing the NDM barbecue, a fight broke out, I would lose in a terrible manner.

From here, it is easy to see how my understanding of the NDM was shaped by gossip and macabre retellings of allegedly committed acts. Sometimes it is easier to believe what we imagine than to accept what we see. My war is punctuated with moments when I refused to view the person before me as a human, another being blessed with a unique blend of qualities. Rather, I saw what Our Dear Leader, our society and my training told me to see: an abomination. Beings whose attempts at mimicking human behaviour filled us with disgust, and made us hate them all the more. These . . . things had no worth. It embarrasses me to say, such was my thinking until recently. Today, the curtain has dropped and the rotten construction is there for all to see.

*

My general apprehension about taking a thumping at the hands of the NDM officers was greatly overblown. During the course of the evening, I discovered that not all members of the NDM were thuggish and crude. Life is filled with small lessons. This one being: second-hand knowledge is no match for what we see with our own eyes.

The men were newly inducted National Defence Movement officers, and the immense barbecue their way of celebration. My arrival added to the general good humour. The officers claimed to have instructed the butterflies to go out and find a suitable guest. By the way, these are the NDM officers' words, not mine! They delivered the information in such a serious tone, I was momentarily fooled, and the resulting confusion written across my face triggered an outburst of laughter. This was followed by a noisy invitation to join their celebrations. There was no escape from the warm clutches of their welcome. I could not deny that, but for their NDM membership, these men appeared as living facsimiles of similarly aged friends, relatives, colleagues and acquaintances. Given I had nothing else planned for the evening, I said, 'Yes, why not?'

Linen-covered tables and accompanying benches were placed around the barbecue in a large, squared-off U formation. It was quite a feast. There was an abundance of beer, wine and various liquors. There was enough meat, fruit and dessert to satisfy a city district's hunger. Did NDM officers have larger stomachs than other human beings?

Sometime later, with the sun long gone, I was deep into a debate about the merits of a film currently playing in the city's largest cinema. My debating partner, sitting to the left, disagreed and countered my praise with well-reasoned arguments. My brain was forced to think fast and push hard. In the middle of our back and forth, a voice from across the table moved our discussion to the side and asked: 'What do you have against the National Defence Movement?'

It is possible my mouth fell open as some part of me asked: What kind of question is that? Why here? Why now? Another part recalled how, during an awkward moment at a wedding reception, a distant aunt told me that every decent get-together has a 'serious intermission'. The classification was her own invention, and referred to the moment when light chatter stepped back and allowed 'the serious stuff' to take centre stage. The NDM officers' barbecue was a decent get-together. It had also grown very still. All was silent but for the sizzling meat, and the crickets.

I looked up and expected to see the kind of character who, in the hopes of being <u>provocative</u>, begins to harass other dinner guests with annoying questions. That was not the case. The man at the other side of the table had materialized out of the night air. He had not been there five minutes ago.

It took a few seconds. I recognized him. Back during university days, from time to time we literally crossed paths on campus. We never spoke: he was always over there, and I over here. When we passed, the greeting was usually a simple nod: a neutral acknowledgement of the other.

Bumping into him at the barbecue conjured up a couple of old memories about his permanent 'correctness'. Imagine someone who, whenever you see them, is always in the act of doing or saying the right thing. That is how I saw him back then. He was a fascinating person to watch. I once saw the man hold open a door for a pair of junior students. He did so with such style, as if he was <u>honoured</u> to make way for the others. In fact, I was so impressed with that move, it influenced the manner in which I allow others to pass before me. Another small thing you now know. Something else, and this happened on many occasions while on the way from A to B: a burst of laughter would ambush my thoughts. In reflex I looked up, and who would I see, surrounded by a flock of students? My man, glowing in the adoration that comes with saying the right thing. Now, five years later . . . here he is, asking what ill feelings I harbour towards the NDM!

He explained there was no right or wrong answer to the question. I should see it as an invitation to speak from the heart, and without fear. 'You are a guest at our table,' he said. 'Not an enemy. Here you are safe. Do you understand?' I nodded.

Perhaps the wine had some part to play in my uncharacteristic lack of caution. On the other hand, he did ask for the truth . . . I shared my experience of the twenty-nine gunshots on live radio. I expressed how the incident coloured my views of the NDM. I also mentioned the constant rumours about NDM members' violent behaviour.

He neither dismissed nor laughed at my words. My man nodded slowly, and then said: 'I understand. Truly. Such a violent, yet necessary, break with the old ways would horrify most. However, before shedding tears for those twenty-nine jackals, remember how many citizens died on unsafe roads, or in poorly equipped hospitals, or from hunger or depression. The result of those scoundrels' behaviour. Only gangsters treat their fellow countryfolk in this manner.' He then asked me to compare the nation today with life under the old guard. While doing so, I might also care to check how many times I had witnessed members of the National Defence Movement carrying out aggressive or violent acts. I did as asked . . .

There was no comparison between the old and the new. That was the truth. Most of us were much better off under the NDM. As for the rumoured acts of NDM thuggery, they remained but rumours. Whenever I spotted NDM members about town, they were either minding their own business or helping others. I had not witnessed a single act of brutality. This would happen in due course.

'All right,' I said. 'We are better off. And those rumours about violent deeds . . . Well, I have not personally witnessed any such actions.'

My man shrugged and said, 'That's all right.' His words had the effect of switching the power back on: we returned to the chatter and laughter of minutes earlier.

I never finished that film discussion. The rest of the

night was spent in conversation with my man across the table. The topics remained light, and ranged from sports to fashion to best beers and, believe it or not, our favourite fairy tales! We shared similar views on a number of matters, albeit from distinct perspectives.

At some point during our rambling conversation, he threw in the question, 'What do you know about the National Defence Movement?'

I thought for a bit, dug around for useful info. There was nothing but gossip. 'Not much,' I admitted.

He flashed an easy-going smile. 'Not a problem. If you truly wish to learn more about the National Defence Movement, I can arrange for a visit to HQ. What are you doing tomorrow?'

Tomorrow? Had my man invited me to an aircraft or pottery factory, a bank headquarters, a garment studio . . . instant acceptance would have been my response. But the National Defence Movement Headquarters . . . the Dear Leader . . . twenty-nine gunshots . . . At the same time, I did not wish to come across as hesitant or timid. A matter of ego, perhaps. We agreed to meet in the morning. Eight o'clock. On the steps in front of NDM HQ.

*

As I write, my thoughts are thrown back to an interaction between my nine-and-a-half-year-old self and Father. I stood before a large, well-constructed desk: simple lines, all function. On the opposite side sat Father, watching me. Back then, being much younger and with less life experience, the effect of his gaze was mercilessly uncomfortable. His infinite patience added to the discomfort. Something I had done had received, in my view, an unnecessarily complicated response: I was expected to, one, explain the motivation behind my action, and two, let it be known whether I intended to do this sort of thing for the rest of my life. Could anyone, other than Father, honestly expect a child of my age to have such insight? Father then leaned back in his chair, all the while gazing right through my head. I considered running, but the consequences were too severe and would lead to even more of that withering gaze. 'What will you do tomorrow?' he asked.

Three times, and I remember this clearly, Father tried to extract an answer from me. 'I am not asking for the right answer. I just need an answer. Any kind is good enough!' he said. By this time, I had come to the understanding that answers were extremely dangerous.

4

NDM HQ building was located in the city's East-Central District. As far as I remembered, it had always been home to one government department or another. It was also the least friendly building in the city. No matter how warm and bright the sun, NDM HQ remained cold. The combination of a stern facade and the rows of rectangular windows always set my nerves on edge. I could never shake the feeling NDM HQ watched my every move. The building spooked me to the point where my imagination generated visions of gloomy scenarios involving myself and NDM HQ. None included me walking in through the heavy doors of my own volition. I was usually dragged in screaming. This is why, as you discovered, whenever in this part of town, great efforts were made to avoid NDM HQ and the surrounding area.

That day I arrived forty-five minutes early. My nerves were not in the best of shape. Too much wine, too little sleep. The previous night, accepting the invitation had seemed like an excellent idea, an opportunity to enter the unknown (NDM HQ) and discover what went on inside. That morning, I was reminded once again that the heart of the National Defence Movement lies here. The beating control centre of the machine that lifts the nation and moves us all in a direction of the NDM's choice. As I paced back and forth in front of the dark facade, a small voice within (my conscience perhaps) asked what I was doing there.

Around the time of the NDM officers' barbecue, I struggled with the 'Purpose-in-life Blues'. I was terrified by my choices: was this the right way to go or thing to do? Or what about that? Too many options got in the way. I could try my hand at just about anything, which I did. Though I never stuck at the various activities long enough for my actions to result in anything of value. My uncles saw fit to involve themselves in my business. Such had been their way since Father's death. Whenever I crossed paths with my uncles (by that time a suspiciously frequent occurrence), they began hammering my ears with a hundred and one versions of the same questions. <u>What was I doing? Where was I heading?</u> 'Just trying to help you get out of the rut you are in,' they claimed. If anything, their actions pushed me deeper into the trench.

Their mission, according to Mother, was to help take care of us as Father would have done. In recent years, however, rather than offer any useful wisdom, my uncles engaged in a campaign of personal harassment. There were times I believed my uncles' aim (on the matter of what I planned to do with my life) was to worry and complain harder than their deceased brother, Father, ever had. The previous night was no exception. Without so much as a greeting, they launched into a vicious, two-pronged verbal attack on my lifestyle. They even had the condescending audacity to bring up the young, hyperactive me, the one accused of either having ants in his pants, or some affliction of the nerves. The 'troublesome' one. The one who caused family members to sigh, shake their heads and wonder what would ever become of me. What they hoped to achieve by bringing that up is beyond my understanding. However, my uncles' unnecessary reminder of the past is not what kept me awake for much of the night. Rather, it was a question of theirs: 'Are you committed to anything other than <u>yourself</u>?' As a child I would engage in a game in which I repeated a word for minutes on end. Again and again, until the meaning of the word disappeared, and what remained was a new appreciation of the many noises made by my throat and mouth. The night of the barbecue, my uncles' question behaved in a similar fashion: I heard it again and again. Between the hours of four and five I experienced an unfortunate revelation: so far in this life, I had committed to nothing. The non-committed status had little to do with a principled neutrality. The truth as understood from this position was that I was simply too scared to be bothered. Too afraid to face the possibility of failure, and as a result, my achievements thus far had amounted to nothing. This insight followed me out of bed and accompanied me as I shaved. It was there through coffee and toast, and travelled with me to NDM HQ.

I stopped pacing at 0754, and turned my attention to the stream of uniformed women and men moving in and out through the grand entrance. I watched until patterns emerged. Those heading in greatly outnumbered those coming out. Of course it was morning, and the start of the working day for most. By observing the hundreds of NDM staff, I soon learned to apportion rank according to how much each person carried: the higher the rank, the emptier the hands. I counted five instances in which the level of importance was such that others were employed to do the carrying. I also noticed that everyone, no matter their age, shape or size, walked upright, proud and self-assured. They moved like people who knew how to achieve their life goals. The general appeal of this vibrant energy did not leave me untouched. I felt slow, to the point of moving backwards. My mind threw up two sentences and recited them twice: 'Those with plans move forward. Those without, step back.' My uncles again.

A light tap on my left shoulder. I turned and found my man standing with two colleagues, all smiling. We exchanged greetings. I was introduced, jokingly, as a 'non-believer with a curious soul'. His colleagues (child-hood friends, by the way) said they were honoured by my presence, and hoped I would have an enlightening visit. They also gave me a brief summary of their work within the NDM. To tell the truth, these men could just as well have been discussing the frying of pancakes or the breed-ing of cattle. I heard nothing they said. My eyes and brain focused every gram of attention on their uniforms! Since the NDM takeover, I had become aware of the appear-ance and spread of uniformed characters across the city and country. However, my MO of avoiding NDM mem-bers meant I was never in close enough range to inspect an NDM officer's kit. The three men in their uniforms looked magnificent! Stunning.

Looking back with the benefit of time, I have the feeling my man (goodness knows what has become of him) noticed the effect their uniforms had on my impressionable self. He must have seen how I stared at the fabric, the cut, the colour, the buttons, the belt, boots, insignia, etc. The pride I usually had in my scruffy-casual-intellectual look vanished on the spot. I stood there and felt very much a raggedy soul, committed to nothing.

They say you never know until you <u>look with care</u>. My imagination, and the usually safe distance I kept from the NDM HQ building, had rendered its doors the spiritual boundary between light and darkness. As we walked towards the mighty entrance, the doors transformed into two giant canvases covered in multiple layers of exquisite ironwork. The resulting piece, called 'Forest of Life', was spectacular. Plants, creatures, people and structures, given a magical depth by the morning shadows, told the visual history of the nation. I could have spent an hour studying the work.

We passed through five pairs of double doors on our

way to the official entrance. Each door was significantly larger than the one before, and the effect on the viewer was a shrinking sensation. By the time we arrived at the fifth pair, I felt exceptionally small. The doors opened, and I expected to enter a gloomy hall through which NDM staff moved in dignified silence. Instead, the building delivered a wonderful surprise: I walked into a bright and finely landscaped courtyard garden .

The garden's surface was a series of gently rolling hills in miniature. The fresh green grass was criss-crossed with a network of paths along which NDM HQ staff moved one way and another. A few park benches were scattered around an oval pool at the centre of the garden. From just below the water's surface, a grid of nozzles fired random jets of water at the sky. The trees were arranged in five groups (of shared interests or similar disposition) across the garden. Trees inside a building? Incredible! For a few seconds, I fought a powerful urge to run through the landscape while letting out whoops of youthful joy. How I loved the new and unexpected. Naturally, I controlled myself, and chose the next best option, which was to stare about me with a wide-open mouth.

The surrounding facades (the vertical boundaries of

the garden) were constructed from glass and steel, using a technique I had not seen before. From my position, and because there was so much glass, I could peer deep inside most of the lower-floor offices and observe the goings-on within. NDM members, every one of them fully committed to the nation's glory, went about their business with confidence and efficiency. After what might have been minutes of gawking, we made our way to the official entrance at the opposite end of the garden.

My personal tour of the headquarters involved significant mileage on foot and an almost never-ending series of introductions. We began at my man's office, which handled the strategic analysis of national-security-relevant information. I gathered from the pride with which he spoke that it was one of the NDM's more important departments. We were out and off to other places before I had a chance to discover anything more about national-security-relevant matters.

We dashed in and out of meeting areas. We visited rooms filled with maps and charts. I saw scale model tanks in one workshop, and a collection of model aircraft in another: they were not toys. One section of the building, four or five rooms, was dedicated to formulating and disseminating the NDM's message. Two of the rooms had walls covered in posters: dramatic lines, NDM colours and catchy public-facing slogans. Over the next months, I spotted a number of these posters out and about in the city.

I shook hands with people usually seen in newsreels and newspaper photographs. I was too surprised to remember the expected deference. Thankfully my ill manners were forgiven. One of my visit's highlights was the NDM Library. How I loved the place: the light, the shelves, that familiar 'old book' smell. The one that always made me feel at home. Do you remember when we tried to discover if it was a perfume created and maintained by librarians around the world?

A complex as sophisticated as NDM HQ cannot run on empty stomachs. The kitchen ensured every member of staff (and any guests) received a choice of nourishment to keep the spirits up and the body strong. A variety of healthy and tasty food was served in the great cafeteria, which was another impressive room. Picture a large, triple-height space, marked out by a grid of columns. Suspended a little over halfway up from each of the columns was a circular balcony. My man informed me that these were the prime dining spots. I looked around and understood why: the view. An entire wall of the cafeteria, consisting of floor-to-ceiling glass-and-steel panels, opened onto the garden and blurred the boundary between inside and out. The food was so much better than usual canteen fare. I sat and ate and looked around. As far as I could see, there were only seven of us without uniform, six of whom were impeccably dressed. This probably bothered me more than anyone else. The NDM members taking lunch in the cafeteria radiated joy, camaraderie and confidence. They had more important matters on their minds than my clothing.

In between the trips from one corner of the building to another, I was bombarded with nuggets of information and flashes of opinion. Every word was employed in the explanation of an NDM position or choice. At times I was challenged and asked about my views. Once, quite unexpectedly, my man asked if I was one of those who preferred to let others do the heavy lifting, while watching from a position of comfort. Later on, he asked if I believed my opinions represented the full extent of reason on our globe. At another moment, he speculated whether such an excessively comfortable citizen as myself, insulated from the machinery of society, could ever understand what it meant for the baker to make bread, or how the city remained clean, or how the NDM kept the nation's citizens safe. He always moved on before I could think up an answer. My man also presented me with arguments regarding the necessity of national preparedness. Did I know that, as we spoke, the nation was in peril? Was I aware of the vast army amassed along our western border? Men and materiel of the Western forces, who were certainly not there for farming purposes! Did I not agree our nation had the right to develop the capacity for offensive defence as a deterrent, as would any other nation? I remained silent during such moments. What could I say?

We visited a room unofficially known as 'The Shrine'. A quiet, hallowed chamber, with space for no more than a dozen visitors at a time. A perfect cube, the walls and ceiling of which were covered in padded midnight-blue velvet. There was no natural light. An array of thoughtfully positioned spotlights illuminated a volume encased in glass at the centre of the room. It was the original, handwritten version of the Dear Leader's manifesto! I moved in for a closer look, and noted the man had exceptional penmanship. I read: 'When every member in every quarter of the nation comes together and pulls as one, we can lift ourselves from the stagnant swamp that has been our home for too long. A nation that functions as a single, committed unit can eliminate all obstacles, home-grown or external, that litter the path of progress.'

5

Time must have run at quadruple speed. Without an understanding of quite how, we suddenly found ourselves in the middle of the afternoon. The end of my visit approached. We stood in silence and waited for the lift. Half a day's worth of information had been poured into my eyes and ears. It made me dizzy, and the foundations supporting my understanding of the NDM began to crumble. These cracks developed out of an inability to match what I saw around me with the preconceptions in my head. Of course, it is impossible to learn the truth about anyone or any organization within the space of a few hours. However, as with the officers at the barbecue the day before, there was nothing menacing about NDM HQ. The simple fact was, during my visit I saw and heard nothing to confirm a single one of my suspicions or prejudices. The building spoke to me. There are no adequate words to describe the vibrations emanating from every body and every surface within it. I can say, at the risk of sounding peculiar, the place felt like a home, and it called out a welcome.

The lift stopped at the second floor, and we stepped out. We turned left, and then right, through a short passage that brought us to a vast atelier. It occupied half of the floor. This is where the National Defence Movement's aesthetic was designed and perfected. The atelier was run by NDM Messaging and Public Relations, the same department responsible for the posters I had seen earlier in the day.

We were received by a member of the design team responsible for the officer uniforms. The Head of Design and I did not share the same concept of personal space. She stood close enough for me to feel her body warmth, and hear the air flow in and out through her nostrils. It was a patient sound. She seemed to spend an eternity peering into my head. It was a near spiritual experience, and just before the designer's examination caused the invisible me to float, she asked: 'Who are you?' Eyes are funny and filled with all kinds of information. They are often the starting point for unusual events. Who was I? I gazed into the designer's round, brown eyes. A quiet flash.

*

The designer coughed gently. I smelled oranges or tangerines, and blinked myself back into the atelier. Had I been staring at her all the while? I looked at my man. A gentle smile, nothing more. I had drifted away. My man chimed in with the suggestion last night might have been rather heavy on the liver. The Head of Design sighed, and then said: 'Please try to pay attention.' I apologized, and then listened with a determined focus as she explained the atelier's workings. In order to stave off the onset of boredom, and to encourage a holistic understanding of the creative process, from sketched-out idea to finished product, staff were rotated from one section to another every three months.

I looked around the atelier. Everyone present was engaged in one of the component processes: sketching, cutting, pressing, sewing, etc. A good number of the activities were alien to my eyes. What struck me most of all was the focus and efficiency applied to the work. Every move and every action appeared deliberate and natural to the task at hand. Did those who designed and built machines draw their inspiration from places such as this? As the designer spoke, a young man with an off-white tape appeared and began measuring various sections of my structure. I was told not to worry. This happened swiftly and with minimal interference. Measurements done, the young man spun around and walked out of the room.

The Head of Design concluded her presentation with a brief lesson on the evolution and multiple functions of the uniform. One of which was to serve as an integral element in the 'Aesthetic of the Moment'. This was a concept developed by the Dear Leader. 'In a time where our actions are increasingly recorded through photography and motion film, the uniform plays a significant role in shaping the world's view of our nation.' The Head of Design, who had memorized every word, delivered the full three-minute manifesto. She quoted the Dear Leader with joy. Or was that love?

In conclusion, before leaving the room, the Head of Design thanked me for listening. I thanked her for an enlightening presentation. Seconds later, the man who measured me returned with a team of five assistants. They took up positions around me. One held a pair of grey socks and a set of blue and white underwear. Another carried in one hand a black cotton shirt and tie, the other hand cupping a small bowl, half-filled with brassy-looking bits and pieces. One assistant carried a jacket. Another, a pair of trousers and a wide canvas belt, the buckle of which was simple and functional, without engraving or other orna-mentation. The last assistant gripped a rectangular tray, on which stood a pair of shiny black boots. I recognized these as the components of an NDM officer uniform. What did they have to do with me?

My man noted my confusion and assured me all was good and well. He did, however, have a confession to make. While it was true, our acquaintance was less than a day old, certainly not enough time to fully assess the character of another or begin to understand them, he had, during the hours of my tour and during last night's barbecue, picked up on a certain resonance. A particular honesty, openness and wit . . .

His compliments tickled my ego and my chest tingled with pride, especially when he said: 'You know . . . There is something in you. Underneath all this scruffy business . . .' An up-and-down wave of the hand made reference to my attire. 'I catch a glimpse of officer material.' My body received a compliment as well: my man claimed I had the perfect size and shape, almost as if I was born to carry an NDM officer's uniform! Furthermore, given my educa-tion, there would be no need to join the Movement at the lower ranks. Were I to choose the NDM, I could step in at officer level. 'And trust me,' he said, 'there are certain benefits that come with the NDM officer class.' My man stepped forward and began to tempt my ears with an impressive and irresistible list of all I stood to gain. As I listened, odd shifts occurred within me. It felt like preparation. The recital ended, leaving me in no doubt about how well the NDM looked after its own. 'The choice is entirely up to you,' he said. 'I think you should, at the very least, give the opportunity some consideration.' I learned that because he saw me as an open-minded fellow, and understood how such considerations might present a challenge, he had taken the liberty of requesting a uniform fitting. I should see it as a little 'thinking assistance'. It was a straightforward agreement. I was free to take the uniform and wear it about town for a week. There were no strings attached, other than the obligation to treat the uniform with care, make notes on my experiences while wearing it and, on return, share my observations with the design team.

I was then asked to remove my clothes. All of them. My first thought was that I had misheard. But, after a few seconds of disbelief, the request was repeated. That is correct, they expected me to strip naked in front of everyone! I took a few moments to consider. Perhaps it was my pride, or a strong desire not to come across as insecure. Usually such a demand would result in my telling someone to go and jump in a lake. Yet on that afternoon, meek as a lamb, I followed instructions. To my surprise, and deep gratitude, no one looked. It was a unique and slightly amusing experience. There I was, standing, birthday naked, in the middle of a room on the second floor of NDM HQ and no one cared!

You once asked what I believed were the three most important elements of clothing. 'A good piece of clothing,' I told you, 'contains, comfort, more comfort, and even more comfort.' Well, the NDM uniform was the most comfortable, best-fitting cloth to ever wrap itself around my skin. I turned one way and then the other, moved my arms around, stepped forwards, backwards . . . No matter how I contorted my body, the uniform's fabric moved with me, no resistance whatsoever. At the risk of sounding like one whose mind has run away, I clearly remember the uniform and my spirit taking an instant liking to one another. They fused together and formed a beautiful shell. There is no other way to describe the sensation: pure beauty!

The moment of joy was interrupted by a touch on my shoulder. I turned and found the man who had measured me beckoning with his left hand. 'This way,' he said. I was led to a mirrored wall where I received a simple set of instructions: 'Take your time, sir. Admire yourself.'

Thoughtless. Speechless. How do I describe that first impression? Speaking without exaggeration, were it possible to fall in love with oneself I would have done so then and there. I gazed at my reflection. The world around me vanished. Who <u>was</u> that man? He looked familiar. Picture a radiant version of myself who, though clad in black, gave off a light that bounced out of the mirror and reverberated in my stomach and chest. It glowed within my heart, at my fingertips, and along every nerve. Looking back, I now understand what happened in that moment. The old me stepped out from my static cocoon, the new me opened my wings and prepared to take flight.

I remember the energy released during that moment as phenomenal. It brought to mind an incident from many years ago. As I wandered through the spring meadows, just beyond the city's eastern boundaries, six or seven stampeding horses appeared out of nowhere and practically gave me a heart attack. The size. The noise. Their power! The lady who looked to be in charge said I had no reason to worry: the horses were simply happy to be out running for the first time in a while. Dressed in the NDM officer's uniform, I felt a thousand such horses run through me. I grew inside, though not as a balloon inflated with hot air: my new volume had substance. I stared at me in the mirror and saw glory. My flesh tingled and became hot. A result of the friction taking place within. My soul, it changed shape. Back then, of course, it all felt so wonderful. I was a beautiful sight. Near perfect. The one blemish, if we may call it that, was the shadow that flickered in the eyes of my reflection.

Once, long ago, I heard one of Mother's friends claim to have become afraid of herself. They were involved in what I called 'grown-up' talk. However, the concept of being afraid of oneself fascinated my young mind, and I spent a few weeks, without success, thinking how best to achieve such a condition. Had this memory come to mind as I stared in the mirror, would I have recognized the true darkness of the shadows in my eyes, and become afraid? As it was, I did not. Instead, I gazed and admired my glorious self. Oh how my spirit grinned. It felt reborn. You know, along the way, I sometimes wondered how a combination of colour, cloth, cut and shiny leather boots could bring about such transformation. Today, I believe the answer is because I am an ordinary man, filled with basic desires. I wished for a uniform, and now I am here.

I left NDM HQ clad in magnificent black. My 'test' uniform bore no official insignia other than the NDM emblems integral to its design. It gave me no rank and no particular position. However, as I meandered through the city, it did not take long for the uniform's effects to become apparent. A change, though not so much within myself (that metamorphosis had already taken place, back in the NDM atelier), but in the public's reaction to my presence. There was a new deference that took some getting used to. I received an automatic right of way, everywhere. For example, as I casually approached the doors of a department store, a man (a good twenty years my senior) grabbed his partner (also of similar age) as she entered the door. She was just as surprised as I, when her man scolded her for failing to notice my presence and let me through. I offered to wait for them to go through the door, but the gentle, polite style I borrowed from my man failed to work in that particular instance. The man kicked up such a fuss, the only way I could get the couple to walk in first was by invoking imaginary authority. Everywhere, people stood back to let <u>me</u> through. It was an unusual yet pleasant experience.

At one point I entered a park without knowing why I was there. To my right, a hive of primary school children were chaperoned by three ladies who oozed experience and self-control. I watched them pass, every one of them staring wide-eyed and open-mouthed. It was all too much for the second to last child, who broke ranks and ran up to me. His actions provoked an instant reaction from the rest of the class (minus the chaperones). Within seconds I was surrounded by a buzzing, cheerful crowd of children, filled with laughter and brimming with questions. Was I a soldier? Where was my rifle? Was I a general? Did I have a tank? The adoration and attention felt very good. My spirits received a much-needed shot of vitality.

I walked for hours, catching smiles and gracious nods from the citizens. Their attitude (and this memory could be distorted by time and circumstance) suggested I was a different kind of being. They gazed up, I looked down. Was it true, the uniform transformed me into a man of higher status? A better man? A greater man? It felt this way as I experienced the world on that first afternoon dressed in NDM officer kit.

Ah, I can still see the burst of surprise that lit up your face when I arrived the next morning. You were intrigued, claimed the uniform made me look 'interesting', and could not wait to ask your friends for their opinions. The rest of your family, on the other hand, were clear in their approval of my new attire. And my family . . . Father, long dead, was unable to comment and Mother was still too busy with grief. My younger sisters looked, shrugged and then asked how I could possibly be a soldier without a gun.

The uniform allowed me to feel a new range of sensations. Previously dormant parts of my being awoke and prepared for action. Potent and powerful. From where I sit now, it is easy to think of the old tales where adorning oneself with a particular attire, or using a specific tool, led to the capture (or destruction) of the soul. There are truths in those ancient myths. Two days after my trip to NDM HQ, I signed up for officer training. You supported my new and unexpected allegiance to the NDM, and my need to explore what it meant to commit to a belief. Though you also warned me to remain wary of the power of collective thought. I laughed at that and professed to know what I was doing. Your questions and occasional comments made it clear you never fully accepted my reasons for joining up. You were right. The reasons I gave were feeble and built upon shaky foundations and big talk. I lied because I feared your reaction. I was too ashamed to admit my move in this direction was not driven by philosophical insight or the need to commit. The motivation to join the NDM was driven by nothing more than a desire to keep hold of what the uniform gave me: love, respect and authority. That was all it took to turn my head and send me along this disastrous path.

On the matter of our training, there was one class called 'Self-Identification'. I never discussed it before because we were explicitly forbidden from doing so. The lessons in this class were for the elite and no one else. In truth, it was, and still is, difficult to view the happenings in Self-Identification as lessons. Our sole activity was to chant a number of carefully selected mantras for various lengths of time. I honestly planned to tell you about this class one day, when circumstances allowed. Well, here we are . . .

On the day of our final class, two hundred and twenty-five of us stood erect, arranged in a fifteen-by-fifteen grid, three paces apart. Our location was a large aircraft hangar. At the far end of the space, the hands of a large clock mounted on a white panel indicated thirteen minutes past five in the morning. Before us a stocky sergeant, more bear than man, stood legs apart in the manner of a conqueror. He barked out a question: 'What are you?' We officer cadets replied with a resounding: 'I am a God!' 'What are you?' he roared. 'I am a God!' we thundered. 'What are you?' 'I am a God!' Initially the timing of our replies was a bit rough. Some of the men shouted out a touch too early, or a shade too late. Though by 0600 our voices had fused into a synchronized rhythm.

'What are you?' 'I am a God!' 'What are you?' 'I am a God!'
'What are you?' 'I am a God!' 'What are you?' 'I am a God!'
'What are you?' 'I am a God!' 'What are you?' 'I am a God!'
'What are you?' 'I am a God!' 'What are you?' 'I am a God!'
'What are you?' 'I am a God!' 'What are you?' 'I am a God!'
'What are you?' 'I am a God!' 'What are you?' 'I am a God!'
'What are you?' 'I am a God!'

I repeat these words in the hope you can understand the madness of our situation. 'What are you?' 'I am a God!'

Again and again and again. The sergeant barked, and we screamed in reply. Our longest chanting session in the Self-Identification class had been three hours. On the final day of class we roared through that record with ease. 'What are you?' 'I am a God!' 'What are you?' 'I am a God!'

1100. A man on the left, close to where I stood, collapsed. He fell to the ground and was quietly removed. The muscles in our necks and throats were on fire, and had been so for a while. Our lungs begged for mercy. Our bones were shaken by the roar of our own thunder. 'What are you?' 'I am a God!' Whatever kept us going came from somewhere beyond ourselves.

1230. Agony and a deep, deep hatred of the sergeant. A few more men were removed. We found strength and perseverance in oneness. Meanwhile, my mind was not happy and threatened to climb out of my body. My ears heard what was not there. Donkeys! Mad donkeys. Thousands of screaming donkeys. But there were no donkeys in this space, only screeching officers-to-be. 'What are you?' 'I am a God!'

1310. I spent the last quarter of an hour wishing for sleep or death. Anything but the chanting. My body despised me for putting it through such torment. It was not my fault. Something else was in control. Our shouts were now driven by force of habit, and none of us could stop the noise erupting from our throats. 'What are you?' roared the bear. 'I am a God!' we screamed.

They say, just before the moment of death, a film of our lives plays out in the theatres of our minds. Obviously no one living can say whether or not this is true. I can, however, tell you (based on personal experience) that being trapped in the prison of one's final hours adds a vibrancy to the memories. As I now remember, at 1335, as our vocal cords prepared to die and our bodies collapse, we felt a light.

The sun threw down a beam. It erased our pain, removed our suffering, and replaced them with a sense of supremacy over every other being. We felt the change of status in our flesh, in our bones, our hearts and minds. The agony and fatigue were gone. With our feet planted firmly on the ground, our spirits rose metres into the air as our chanting elevated us into a state of collective ecstasy. There was no longer any need for the sergeant's question. The chant 'I am a God! I am a God! I am a God!' thundered around the aircraft hangar for another hour and thirty minutes.

Meanwhile, in the world around us, the armies massing along our western borders built up an aggressive momentum. There was nothing friendly about their presence. A radio reporter described the Western Armoured Divisions as 'fields of cats, waiting to pounce'. The language employed in communications between the Dear Leader and the Head of the West sharpened in tone. Unfortunately, neither man was able to hear the other. Pride is a stubborn and meddlesome force. Vicious polemics flew back and forth between our capitals. The angry poison trickled down and spread across the fields and streets. It touched us all. We no longer asked if war was coming. We wondered when.

Ah! A last-minute intervention at the behest of our bordering nations. The two leaders flew off to neutral territory and engaged in urgent talks aimed at defusing an explosive situation. The radio and the papers inserted words such as 'De-escalation' and 'Compromise' and 'Reason' into their headlines. For seven tense and infinitely long days, the Dear Leader 'negotiated'. The nation waited, breathless. A few of us noticed Hope pack its bags and head for safety.

6

War arrived during the second month of officer training. Early in the afternoon on the eighth day of peace talks, a flood of noisy chatter from the West claimed one of our units had broken through the border and attacked their troops. There were no NDM units in the vicinity of the alleged assault. We relayed this knowledge to the West, together with an urgent request for them to check their information again. In reply: disconnected lines of communication and white noise. Hours later we learned that a truckload of our well-known <u>situational artists</u>, in a bout of drunken foolishness, had crossed the border and hurled paint at Western army tanks. Apparently they wanted to make a <u>statement</u> of sorts. The unfortunate artists did not leave behind a note, and the deeper thinking contained within their statement was never known. The artists never discovered the wider repercussions of their actions. The Western delegation viewed the tossed paint as an insult to their armed forces and their nation. Such a deliberate and violent provocation could not be tolerated.

They swore our attack would be avenged. The Western negotiating delegation's response was needlessly dramatic: they stormed out of the talks and flew back to their capital. Our people were stunned, describing the Westerners as 'crying like a nursery of spoiled infants over a few splashes of paint'.

The Western leader was a weak man with a rotten spirit. He also had an ability to find personal insult and mischief lurking in every shadow on the ground, every cloud floating above, and certainly in a spot of paint. He was noisy, and we joked that his bark could be heard on the other side of the globe. He loved attention, and appeared happiest when showing off his latest excessive vanity project to adoring crowds. It is on record that their leader had paid followers! They went everywhere with him, cheering his every word and action. In the meantime, he, together with a select group of friends, plundered and squandered their land's wealth as if it were a personal cache of gold.

The Western leadership were a malfunctioning bunch, with nothing but corruption and a large, angry army to show for decades of rule. The rapid and enthusiastic embrace of war served as a convenient distraction: a well-known, often-used move. We saw through our neighbour's flimsy excuse for a declaration of war. The Western attack was driven by a case of sour grapes. The NDM's rise to power, together with its anti-corruption practices, put an end to the multiple kickback schemes established between the Western leadership and our since dispatched government. We hurt their wallets, and so they attacked. However, far more damaging than the bullets, bombs and shells was the West's treachery. We had once been such happy neighbours.

The result of our not-quite-ready military status was a series of heavy defeats. Worried voices asked why the NDM leadership had not tried harder to achieve a peaceful resolution. Those voices were few, and quickly shut down with a reminder that 'you cannot make peace with treacherous souls'. In the meantime, our neighbours to the north and east, perhaps sensing blood or an opportunity for profit, introduced irrational trade tariffs and other border-related hindrances. International shipping declared our southern ports 'unsafe' and rerouted their vessels to less volatile locations. Uncertainty and manic hoarding became the order of the day.

In addition to the slow strangulation of the nation and steady loss of our westernmost lands, we received a new gift from our enemy: fear. The confusion of war let the truth about our defeats evolve into a series of increasingly exaggerated tales and rumours. The Western forces were transformed into an invincible <u>monster</u>. One that was heading our way. A monster that, on closer inspection, was no more than the brutal and deadly combination of men and their machines. Unfortunately fear blocked much of our thinking. We used rumours and lies to build a terrifying version of the truth. Fear also gnawed at the bonds holding the nation together. We began to fall apart. The pillars of rationality, common sense and organization crumbled. Have you ever watched a herd of sheep panic? Some dash this way, others run that way, some become locked in a paralysis of indecision that keeps them planted to the spot. The initial phase of the war with the West was marked by nationwide chaos, which brought out the darker side of our survival instinct. Civility and compassion were kicked into the bushes. Even Nature seemed affected by the conflict: the wind hissed with increased aggression, birdsong became angry and shrill. Meanness and mistrust ran free. The idea of 'us' fell out of fashion. In its place appeared an obsessive focus on the 'me'.

*

Not all of us had the courage to remain. Those with the inclination, and means, packed what they could and fled. I understood their reasons for running (we all wish to live), but still found it unfair. We were taught that survival is a reward for the fittest. During those days, it appeared fitness was determined by the size of one's cash reserves. I watched one family after another scurry off until, one day, time ran out for all attempting to flee. I remember that moment well . . .

I had a few free days, and opted to spend them with Mother and my sisters. Mother was her familiar introverted self, and left me unsure whether she was happy to see me or not. My sisters, on the other hand, radiated joy and enthusiasm at my presence. They attacked me with a full battalion of queries about officer training, questions that had clearly been gathered in preparation for my appearance.

At 0420, the sound of excited voices in the street woke me up. I climbed out of bed, walked to the window . . . it was the family opposite. They had piled an impossible amount of luggage into their car. I watched them hug everyone in the small crowd that had gathered, before climbing in (three children in the rear, mother and father in front) and driving off. That the vehicle agreed to move was a miracle in itself! Two hours later, while enjoying my morning mug of coffee, those same neighbours reappeared, luggage and all. Their faces were so sad, and scared. At the behest of the Western leadership, the surrounding nations had sealed their borders, and also denied us access to their airspace. All routes and passages out of the country were closed. I heard months later, by way of my sisters, that the family had missed the border cut-off by fifteen minutes. En route to the airport, they were forced to make three stops because the terrified father's driving gave the children the most awful motion sickness. Wartime and tales of misfortune are very good friends.

The nation was trapped and alone. The worried voices grew louder, and this time no one shut them down. There was no hiding the daily funerals. Men too young to die, but dead nevertheless. Rumour had it, many of the sealed coffins were filled with ballast, as the battlefield had eaten the bodies. The nation trembled. The nation prayed for miracles. The Dear Leader responded. He spoke to us with the voice of a lion. Here, on the edge of ruin and death, I still hear those words. I remember how they straightened our backs, and filled every heart in the land with courage . . .

'The West, once a trusted friend, has shown its true self. They are not brothers and sisters, but a pack of mad dogs who run wild over our beautiful lands. I hear your voices ask: Why have we died at their hands? Why do they consume our territory with such abandon? Why do we absorb blow after blow after blow? The answer, my people, is as simple as it is unfortunate: we were not prepared.' Nothing the Dear Leader said was news to our ears. But we listened all the same. We were calmed by his simple honesty, and the fact he did not treat us as fools.

'Today, I come with good news.' The Dear Leader paused for a few seconds. 'Our forces are now able and ready to remind these gangsters from the West who we are!' The Dear Leader spoke to the nation of our warrior ancestry: 'Deep within every man, woman and child in the land is a warrior. A fighter!' The Dear Leader then commanded us to seek out this fighting spirit within ourselves, and set it free. 'Let it become the wind that blows the enemy dirt back from whence it came.' I have a recollection of listening and feeling a tingling sensation spread over my skin. Whether this was a mere coincidence, or the symptoms of the effect of the Dear Leader's words, I cannot say.

'A family is stronger than one who stands alone,' he said. 'As a nation, as a family, our strength has no bounds. There are no limits to what we can achieve. Citizens of the hamlets, villages, towns and cities in our beautiful nation, bound together by geography, language, culture and our collective histories, let us be one! As one single united family, we shall stop the enemy. We will drive those dogs from our lands and remove every last trace of their existence from our soil! My mothers, my fathers, sisters, brothers, my daughters and sons, it is time to fight!' The Dear Leader spent the next quarter of an hour setting out his vision for our path to victory. His love for the nation moved every one of us. The hollows in our chests filled with a determined fire.

The inspirational effects of the Dear Leader's speech were reflected in the radio and paper headlines, and also in the general demeanour of the nation's citizens. Across the country, here in the city, we began to hear stories about quarters of society coming together and unexpectedly rediscovering cooperation, sharing and mutual protection. During this period there was also an increase in the number of new faces on the city's streets. The newcomers were easy to spot. It was in their eyes and facial expressions: an unsettled, haunted shock. It was there to see in the peculiar way many had of moving from A to B, as if trying to evade invisible hunters. We welcomed them and provided comfort where possible. In those days, I had to try to imagine what events could paint such horror onto a face. Back then.

In the meantime, the officer training programme intensified. Leisure became ancient history. Ever-increasing portions of our time were devoted to studying battlefield tactics and the like. Increased emphasis was placed on flexibility and improvisation.

Two weeks after the Dear Leader's rousing speech, the enemy's march into our land came to a halt. The Westerners were taken aback by our new-found will to resist at all costs. Our armies remained frozen for a month. We made good use of the time afforded by the stalemate to manoeuvre ourselves into an advantageous position. Once NDM High Command determined all was ready, we struck. Our forces, supported by the nation's courage, began to move west. Buds of cautious optimism bloomed.

There was pride and joy as our unconventional battle methods terrified and scattered the Western troops. We reduced them to a broken, frightened mob. Decimated and humiliated on the battlefield, the enemy began a retreat. It quickly evolved into a rout.

My position and circumstances during officer training gave me access to a stream of insider information. This was primarily due to my trainee posting to NDM High Command, which occupied the whole of the top floor of the once feared NDM HQ. I was now one of them, and the building had become a second home.

I was tasked with clerical matters that mostly consisted of map preparation. Not cartography, rather the preparation of the maps employed during various strategic meetings. When performed as expected, mine was an invisible function. This <u>transparency</u> allowed me to listen in on the sounds of military success. Those sounds increased in volume as it became clear the Western armies had no response to our renewed fighting spirit. We thought faster, and fought harder. The strong erased the weak.

A side note about my time with the maps. There was a particular trio of senior officers at NDM High Command who were nowhere near as competent as their rank implied. Areas within their brains usually reserved for reason and common sense had quite probably been displaced by ego. The senior men could not understand what they saw on the maps, and rather than admit this in front of their colleagues, they used me as a vent for the fury ignited by embarrassment caused by their ignorance. In response to this frequent harassment, I developed a map data coding system comprising coloured dots and blocks. It allowed the trio to understand what they saw on the maps, and do so in a manner that made them look smart. It also kept them off my back.

The latter phase of my posting, as we approached the moment of victory, was especially interesting. I was present during five heated discussions (perhaps shouting contests is a better description). The NDM High Command debated the pros and cons of halting our advance at the border, or pushing on to capture Western territory. A small clique desperately wished to teach the Westerners a lesson. One to be remembered for centuries. They believed this could be achieved by continuing our forward momentum and destroying everything between our border and their capital city. A larger group cautioned against a loss of focus, and reminded all present that our military goal was the removal of Western forces. The Dear Leader was present during the fifth and final such meeting. I got to see him in the flesh for longer than a passing moment. Photographs and film could not capture the aura of this man. He had an air about him you needed to experience in order to understand.

I watched in awe as the Dear Leader listened carefully to both points of view. With arguments made, he sat in silence, palms together (as if in prayer), head raised, and eyes focused on some point far beyond the ceiling. Eventually, after an exceptionally long two minutes, the Dear Leader took a sip from his glass of water and said: 'War is an unfortunate but necessary horror. Victories are covered in blood and scarred with lost souls. We stop at our borders.' The Dear Leader believed the manner in which we drove the Western forces from our lands was lesson enough. 'Let them surrender,' he said, and received a round of applause from the majority in the room. Those who argued in favour of further conquest struggled to hide their disappointment. One high-ranking officer, in charge of the National Defence Appliance Programme, was so infuriated he lost his composure and began a bulging-eyed song and dance about the need to battle-test certain new weapons systems. The man complained at length about the time and effort and funding spent on the weapons. The Dear Leader nodded patiently, as a parent listens to a rambling child, and then thanked the man for his outstanding efforts. Of course he recognized, and was excited by, the potential of such weaponry. However, with the war as good as won, he saw little benefit in revealing the extent of our military capabilities to others. The new weapons would remain out of sight for the time being. The high-ranking officer had little choice but to sigh and accept defeat.

Annihilation is an ugly word, though it is an honest description of the Western army's fate. An obstinate pride infected the minds of the Western leadership and blinded them to the truth. On four occasions we offered surrender proposals that provided safe passage home for the Western troops still within our borders. Their leaders remained stubborn and did not believe we would punish their forces as we did, until we did just that. The battlefield slaughter cleared the Western leadership's minds, and our fifth proposal was accepted unconditionally. The surrender terms, given what the Westerners had done to us, were generous and fair, an exercise in restraint.

7

Peacetime. The Dear Leader's compassion towards the Westerners, in which he made clear our quarrel was with their leaders, and not with the citizens, had the additional effect of shaming the Western leadership and turning their people against them. Constitutional shifts and impeachment proceedings soon removed the old guard. Thankfully, the transfer of power occurred without the live radio horror our nation had experienced. The guilty received lengthy prison sentences during which they were free to reflect upon their deeds.

The new Western leadership, the polar opposite of the previous overlords, believed in progress and prosperity through mutual cooperation. A renewed emphasis was placed on our nations' common interests. New channels of communication opened wide, and reciprocal agreements were signed: our nations declared they would do everything in their power to prevent a repeat of the recent past. The devastating results of a communication breakdown were only too visible in every town between our midwest and the Western border. The rubble, the shattered spirits, the haunted eyes. Too much sorrow.

As for the lands to our north . . . a state of excellent relations was restored. We signed similar trade and diplomatic agreements to those made with the Westerners. All would have been good and well, were it not for the Easterners' brooding, unforthcoming stance. Communication, when it occurred, was strained and prickly. The relationship between our two nations soon devolved into one of 'necessary accommodation'. International trade did resume, and the border regions regained their natural hustling, bustling way of life. As before, we purchased essential raw materials from our neighbours and fed these to our many industries. The resulting variety of finished products were exported to the lands around us, including the East. All was just as before, but for that cloud.

As the wise often say: 'Silence carries its own message'. The Eastern reticence had us pondering their true intentions. Theirs was not the behaviour of a happy neighbour. What were they thinking? What were their plans? It was impossible to know as we barely spoke. The only information we had regarding the Easterners' position was their persistent and polite refusal to engage in high-level communication: they claimed all was fine between our nations, and further discussions unnecessary. Our response to Eastern behaviour, led by the Dear Leader, was to order all relevant officials to develop a contingency plan. One part of the plan included instructions to quietly build up a stockpile of essential raw materials. Another part of the plan asked for the nation's top strategists to come together to map out a route that would afford us maximum protection.

A lesson learned from the recent conflict was the importance of understanding what the world around us thought at any given moment. With this in mind, the NDM created the Ministry of Data and Security, and blessed it with an instruction guide filled with empty pages. The rules governing what was deemed acceptable practice within the Ministry of Data and Security were viewed as a work in progress. The blank pages would eventually be filled with a compilation of 'field observations'. Since there were no financial reference points for such an undertaking, the new ministry was given an ample and flexible budget.

The Ministry of Data and Security took form and quickly evolved into two divisions, one being External

Data and Security, known as the EDS. Their task was to collect all available information regarding conditions in our neighbours' systems (political, economic, military), and then translate the data into useful intelligence. The EDS were extremely adept at digging up information, no matter how well hidden, and during their first three months of operation brought to light a number of interesting matters. For instance, they discovered one of the primary reasons for our Eastern neighbour's behaviour: disappointment and a festering bitterness with regard to our victory over the Westerners. This, in turn, was connected to the contents of a secret, and quite despicable, agreement signed between the Easterners and the previous Western government. Following our expected defeat, the West and East planned to take joint control of our nation's industries and natural resources. Our victory put an end to such hopes. Exactly how the EDS managed to unearth these documents remains a mystery.

Another interesting and related matter: the Eastern economy was in terrible shape. Their public-facing, theatrical extravagance was all a sham, built upon lies and vague promises. Generations of corrupt and thoroughly incompetent officials, behaving in a manner similar to the former Western leaders, had emptied the nation's accounts, thus limiting its ability to progress. The EDS noted ripples of social discontent spreading through the usually calm Eastern society, as the citizens' patience wore thin. Protests against raised fuel and food prices increased in number and size. There was a worrying multiplication in the number of recorded disorderly and seditious acts. The EDS detected whispers that the Eastern leadership's nerves were on edge, and the search was on for an event, a ploy of sorts, to deflect attention away from the effects of internal rot. The memories of the faux attack used as a pretext by the West to declare war were still fresh in our minds. The EDS kept watching.

The Dear Leader, and his deputies at the top of the NDM, used the knowledge gleaned by the EDS to formulate a proposal of financial assistance. It was in our national interest to have peace and calm in the East. Remember, a happy family sees no need to quarrel with their neighbours. Our envoy in the East, following an insulting five-hour wait, presented the proposal, with the very best of intentions. We offered to pay twenty-four months in advance for our projected raw material needs over the next five years. This would allow the Eastern leadership to free up funds for pressing internal matters. We also offered the Easterners a line of financial credit with favourable rates of interest, accompanied by a justifiable demand for exclusive access to their copper and aluminium deposits.

The verbal ferocity of the Eastern response surprised us. They screamed in our direction: What an insult! How dare we treat their nation as if it were a breadline candidate! Of course we meant nothing of the kind. The Dear Leader immediately apologized for any misunderstanding, and then invited the Eastern leadership to our capital for talks. The invitation was slapped aside. The Easterners, according to EDS reports, believed there was more to gain by playing the hapless victim to our domineering merchant of greed. That was not a good sign.

The second division in the Ministry of Data and Security dealt with matters closer to home. It was not unusual to find people from neighbouring nations resident within our borders. This had always been the way of our nation. We accepted the place of one's birth as coincidence, but saw where one lived as a choice. And so our policy towards strangers was one of generous hospitality. Any who chose to live within our borders were welcomed with open arms, treated as equals, and given the same rights as everyone else. The logic behind this approach being that outsiders brought with them a fresh perspective that challenged our own ideas. The difference in cultures, languages, cuisine, etc., forced us to look again at what made us who we were. The result of such continued self-reflection should benefit the nation. The one obligation for our guests was that they follow the 'house rules'. The foundations of this idea were noble, but in practice it fostered an existence closer to 'equal but apart'. There was little close interaction between the various nationalities (the majority of whom came from the East). Encounters were usually limited to trade, or picking up on the rhythm of another language while out and about.

Such openness had a downside. An enemy who spoke in a tongue we did not understand could sprout roots in unexpected places. From such positions they would spread undetected, and by the time their poisonous intentions came to fruition, it would be too late. The recent Western treachery was a case in point: without the assistance of certain Westerners living among us, our wounds might not have been so deep, and the initial stages of the enemy invasion less successful. Equally as important as the need to maintain a watch over our international neighbours, was the need to remain fully informed on the activities of our resident guests. How did they live? Where did they go? What were they thinking? National observation became the remit of the Division of Internal Data and Security, known as DIDS.

The EDS and DIDS came into being as I made plans to head back to civilian life. Boredom was grinding me into the floor. You had no idea that thoughts about leaving the NDM had moved to the forefront of my mind. Today, I wonder whether sharing them with you might have led to a change in direction. I said nothing, and found myself suffocating in a slow-twisting cloud of repetition. How could I work so hard, so diligently, and still get nowhere? I knew the cause: too much peace and no action. It became impossible to define the boundary between my work and mandatory occupational therapy. And my uncles . . . They had stopped harassing me the moment I joined the NDM. But when did a leopard ever change its spots? It did not take long before they began to grumble and moan about my lack of promotion. As if the two of them had nothing better to do with their lives! As I gathered the momentum to leave the NDM, I crossed paths with an old friend. At first glance, it was just another happy, coincidental meeting. Yet by the end of our conversation, I had begun to move in a new direction. Another route, a darker road. It brought me here.

Fate is not a myth. At some point between then and now I learned to believe in its existence. While reflecting on the journey to this point, I notice how my path was marked by a number of odd coincidences. The butterflies that led me to the NDM officers' barbecue, and now this one. On an afternoon, eight months after our victory over the West, I travelled to an out-of-the-way antiquarian in the south-west of the city in order to pick up a hard-to-come-by volume. The seventy-three-year-old book on 'Modern Thought' (you know the one). The owner and I both had a good laugh about its age and title.

With the book in hand, I wandered around, exploring the neighbourhood. Despite being born and raised in this city, I had not only never visited that part of town, I had no idea it existed! The architecture was stern and proper. I imagined the neighbours to be exceptionally well behaved. Though it is possible my perception of the neighbourhood was distorted by personal thoughts on how best to compose my discharge request. A heavy weight of guilt had attached itself to the idea of leaving the NDM. I could neither remove it nor fully understand the reason for its presence.

While meandering about and scratching my head, who should I bump into as I rounded a corner? No one other than my man from the NDM officers' barbecue, and my guided tour of NDM HQ! The last time we met he was heading out to fight the Westerners, and I was about to commence NDM officer training. He radiated the same satisfied glow I had seen on many of those returning from the front. What experiences caused his spirit to light up in this manner?

Growing up, we were taught to always ask about what we did not know or understand. I mentioned the 'glow' to my man. He laughed, and then spent the next two minutes sharing a summary of his battlefield adventures. Among other things, I learned his unit was present during the Western leadership's surrender. My man planned to remember that moment forever. As he spoke, I felt a slight annoyance at having experienced no action at all. While soldiers such as he were out fighting for the nation, I had spent my time playing with maps.

And there was one other matter . . . his uniform. Yes,

uniforms again! In defence, my goodness, I had never seen one cut in this fashion. The attire of an NDM officer is quite pleasing to the eye, but where our uniforms were black, my man's was a dark maroon, and cut from fabric with a high-quality sheen. As for the tailoring: ours was sharp, his was sharper, and complimented with bold brass fittings and a wide dark brown belt of a similar leather to that of his well-polished boots. The breast-pocket buttons were a touch larger than usual for this type of uniform, though not distracting. The centre of each button was engraved with a wide-open eye. Four eyes down the middle of the jacket, one on the left breast pocket and another on the right. Yes, of course, I know it was a trick of the imagination, but those eyes did look at me. They saw <u>into</u> me, and whispered: 'We are watching. We are!' The same eyes also appeared on the embroidered shoulder patches. The result was truly impressive, and I suffered an attack of envy.

My man expressed his surprise at our meeting in that part of the city. 'Believe it or not,' he said, 'I had it in mind to get in touch, and here you are!' He then asked if I had time to spare. I did, and was invited for a drink at a local establishment.

We sat in a quiet section of the bar, each with a mug of cool, frothy beer. My man was born and still lived in the neighbourhood, a few minutes away from his parents. He asked what I was doing in the area. I showed him the book, which was immediately snatched from my hands. He began reading. Two and a half pages later, my man closed the book and returned the volume. 'May I read this, when you are done?' I agreed. He never did get around to borrowing the book.

The next item on our agenda was what I had been up to since our last meeting. 'Nothing to challenge the spirit,' I said, and went on to explain how the suffocating effects of boredom and lack of action encouraged my return to civilian life. My man listened and nodded with understanding. Then he asked: 'Are the butterflies around?' It took me a few seconds to pick up on the reference to the two butterflies that had escorted me to their picnic. 'I am sure they are here in spirit,' he said. 'I believe Fate has intervened and crossed our paths once again.'

He began with the uniform, though not its style, rather what it represented: the Division of Internal Data and Security. In developing the DIDS uniform, NDM Messaging and Public Relations had arrived at new levels in the expression of the power aesthetic. The importance and difference in the mission, methods and attitude of DIDS were communicated through their attire. I wondered whether the Head of Design I met in the NDM HQ atelier had anything to do with this creation. My man had been recruited by DIDS and given a position (with excellent growth prospects) in the Data and Information Extraction section (DIE). As he explained the generalities of his task, I realized a good amount of his glow was due to pride in his work.

The novelty of the Ministry of Data and Security, as well as the build-while-flying nature of its assembly, led to the occasional discovery of problems in need of effective solutions. One such matter was how to make sense of the increasing volume of data streaming in from the EDS and DIDS. Earlier that same day, during an urgent inter-divisional meeting about tackling the information overload, a reference was made to the thinking behind the colour-coded map analysis tools developed during my posting at NDM High Command, created, as you recall, for entirely skin-saving reasons. When my man told those higher up he knew the officer responsible, they ordered him to get in touch with me first thing tomorrow morning. Fate obviously thought: Why wait?

When offered a position at the Data and Information Extraction department, in the Division of Internal Data and Security, of course I said yes. Such was the power and influence of DIDS, within twenty-four hours I had been plugged into the team tasked with developing a method to process, as efficiently as possible, the streams of incoming data.

During my younger years, friends and I often played a game in which we imagined the lives of the people we saw on the street. Where did they live? Who was their mother and father, brother, sister? Where did they buy their clothes and shoes? Where had they gone to school? What books did they read? Which team did they support? And so on. I took the ideas and thinking found in those childhood memories and used them to develop the framework upon which we built the National Registry. Everyone living within our borders had a name, date of birth, a place of residence, education, employment, family, friends, an ethnicity. They had patterns to their movement, consumption, literature, entertainment, health, leisure, politics, etc. The National Registry was devised as a cross-referential database of all the above. It allowed us to build an understanding of an individual or group by studying every facet of their lives.

The first four months in DIE disappeared in the blink of an eye. We spent endless hours pushing and pulling problems apart in search of solutions. Ideas were born, shredded, reborn, adjusted, redeveloped. Time vanished, and did not reappear until the day we presented the results of our efforts to the Dear Leader. He loved our thinking. The DIE team's efforts in the conception of the National Registry were rewarded with promotions for all. Within the DIDS system, I climbed another few steps, and certainly made good use of the increase in salary: an upgrade in lifestyle. You accepted the changes. I loved them. A new house, with room enough for both of us, and more. Yet you did not move in. You <u>were</u> there, sometimes in person, always in spirit. A number of your clothes, shoes and other accessories took up residence at my place. But you never made it your home. I took consolation in your acceptance of the house keys. And yes, I did ask your mother to give you a nudge in the 'moving in' direction. 'Give her time. She is a free spirit,' was her advice. Time . . .

*

The National Registry was set up in conjunction with the 'Health For All' programme. The Dear Leader believed a healthy society was a productive society. And, given the citizens' efforts were of benefit to the nation, it was only decent and fair that the nation took good care of those who made it run. Health For All was an extremely popular programme, as it lowered the barriers usually associated with medical matters. Citizens (nationals and guests) signed up with great enthusiasm, and in doing so, provided the bricks and mortar with which we built our great house of information.

We began cataloguing individuals: name, age, address, nationality, medical history. The 'intakers' were instructed to make the data collection as conversational as possible, to discuss likes, interests, etc. The aim was to avoid unnecessary distress, while gaining a better <u>understanding</u> of the individual. The collated data was drawn from multiple aspects of a citizen's life: records of education, legal and/or criminal matters, financial condition, club and/or union and/or organization membership. The snippets of information were assessed and given specific values. Further examination allowed us to discover predictable patterns and sequences of behaviour. Without going into detail, I can say that we human beings are a very peculiar lot.

The National Registry was an outstanding tool, and within a year was deemed a national treasure and source of pride. On one occasion, the editor of a popular lifestyle magazine, together with a photographic crew, visited the DIE team offices to interview us about our creation. We told her the National Registry was the 'result of a serendipitous coming together of creative, intelligent and analytical minds'.

That was a happy period. Time was shared between us, my work on the National Registry, and ten days of combat training each month. Other than the persistent moodiness of our Eastern neighbours, which was not in itself a cause for alarm, all appeared well.

Ah. Much as I would prefer to complete this train of thought, my presence and attention is required elsewhere. I will return as soon as I can.

8

Bad news, and worrisome too. Our scouts have returned. We sent them out, to the north, south and west, in search of viable passages through the surrounding Eastern forces. The enemy has given them back. All dead. The men were discovered piled on top of one another, in a clearing a little beyond our perimeter. Some of us were deeply shocked and saddened by the sight of our brothers. Others could not comprehend how we failed to spot an enemy crossing the open clearing. They were, after all, carrying dead <u>men</u> not rabbits.

It took us the best part of forty-five minutes to retrieve the bodies. This war has allowed barbarity to run free on all sides, and now, unfortunately, booby-trapping corpses is one of the tactics employed by our adversary. My first experience of this tactic came two months ago, as we retreated west, towards home.

The war had changed, and victory had forgotten about us. Out of the chaos at NDM High Command came orders for our battalion to halt its westward march and move south. Our outnumbered forces had lost control of an Easterner oil refinery in the south of the country. They were driven out with such ferocity and speed, there was not enough time to inflict terminal damage on the structure. 'Send in the Factory Boys' was the general strategic consensus. NDM High Command believed it possible for our Property and Population Control battalion to make tactical adjustments, head south and destroy the refinery. Such a move might have been possible at the start of the war, but not at that moment. Our courage was well placed, but our armies were damaged, and circumstances had turned against us. On the ground, with reality's stench burning the hair in our nostrils, we failed to see the strategic benefits of such action. 'Optics,' said NDM High Command. They brushed aside our point of view, and refused to explain precisely what they meant by optics. We had our orders. The PPC marched south and destroyed the refinery: it was one of many, and a minor one at that. We lost a fifth of our men.

Some hours before leaving the area of the (still intact) refinery, and while searching through the rubble for our dead and wounded, a series of explosions shook our positions. These were not the result of incoming enemy shells.

These detonations were almost gentle, and quite deadly. The enemy was nowhere in sight, yet the search for dead and wounded created <u>more</u> dead and wounded. It took a while before we discovered the Easterners' trick: they had hidden explosive devices in or around the bodies of our dead. This was not the behaviour of a civilized people. I felt disgusted. What manner of poison had infected the enemy's thinking? Allowed them to desecrate a fallen man's body in this manner? Hatred of Easterners flowed through our blood, in vain: we were powerless to avenge these atrocities. On reflection, I wonder how it was possible <u>not</u> to see the hypocrisy of my complaint. The record of my activities up to that point was not a compendium of kindly deeds. Quite the opposite.

In the clearing, we checked the scouts' bodies for hidden explosive devices. They were clean. A cloud, heavy and present in the chest and gut, has descended from the skies above. The death of our three brothers, and the manner of their return makes it clear: there is no way out. There is nowhere to go. There is nothing for us to do but wait. Somewhere out there, beyond the range of our vision, the end approaches.

There were no smiles as I walked around our small patch. Correction. There were a few upwardly curved lips, but the fear in the men's eyes rendered smiles into grimaces. Officer training prepared us for many eventualities. It had not made me ready for this. The best I could do was rest my hand on a trembling shoulder for a quiet moment. 'Make your peace, brother,' I whispered, and then moved on.

It was a short trip. An odd one too. I studied the men. Some appeared locked in reflective pose. I watched others pray: to each their own. There were shivering boys, still green, thrown into the middle of the meat-grinder without the necessary training, and with no useful experience. Their stares ask nervous questions: Is this true? Am I really here? Their faces cry out for Mummy and Daddy to come and rescue them. I encourage these children to accept circumstances as they are. We have no other choice. Some weep. Others are struck by flashes of strategic genius, and advise me on how best to extricate our necks from the enemy's noose. They tell me where to move the troops, and how best to do so. I ask them to look around at the truth: we are all that is left. We <u>are</u> the troops. They stare back at me as if I am the Devil, and then declare, with the certainty of madmen, that reinforcements are on the way. They can feel our saviours' arrival in their bones.

These are strange hours. Yesterday, I would, without hesitation, have berated these men for such expressions of weakness. Today, all I have for them are words of comfort. Whether the noises I make are of any use is anyone's guess.

Thankfully, the majority of the men have pushed their fears and worries to one side. There is meaning to this uniform of ours: honour and courage. We are duty-bound to act befittingly. With braces of steel stiffening their spines, and a final burst of valour flowing through their systems, the men prepare. Yes, our end will be a noisy affair.

I remember reading an article about the experiences of people who had narrowly escaped death. One gentleman claimed his sense of smell improved by a factor of five. A woman was said to have discovered new layers to any music she heard. Another man swore he saw more colours than before. At the time, I found the article amusing. I now stand corrected. The knowledge of a fast-approaching end can intensify one's perception. As I walked through our encampment I discovered an ability to instantly absorb every detail of every face. The curve of ears, the flare of nostrils, the intertwine of eyebrow hairs, a mole, a scar, a field of stubble, a tear, a furrowed brow, eyes focused on a faraway place, a tongue soothing parched lips . . . I do not recall ever looking at faces in this way. You see what circumstances can do to the mind?

But I was writing about my time at DIE . . .

Our development projections had been far too conservative. We put the National Registry together at lightning speed, a rate that exceeded everything we imagined. The NDM leadership expressed their continued satisfaction with our endeavours by increasing the budget, and giving us licence to do whatever it took in order to get the job done. Protecting the nation was a vital task, and all obstacles in our path were removed. The NDM leadership rewrote sections of the National Law in order to accommodate our methods. Exciting days indeed.

Infinitely more rewarding than the results of office work, and a source of great personal joy, was the public's reaction to my uniform as I walked through the city. I wore the uniform of a National Defence Movement officer in the Division of Internal Data and Security. It gave me almost magical powers, setting those of us who wore it above and apart from all other citizens. You saw how it transformed me into an elite human being. I was met with reverence and joy, and suspect the citizens' behaviour was driven by DIDS' reputation as the 'Guardian of the Nation'. You, on the other hand, asked whether their conduct was the result of collective delirium. 'It is just a uniform. It is cloth,' you said. I probably smiled and reminded you how our work helped establish an environment of watchful safety, one that allowed citizens to go about their daily business free from worries. Only a select few would ever wear this cloth, members of the public knew this and were not at all shy about expressing their appreciation.

You and I reacted to this in quite opposite ways. You found it uncomfortable, unnatural, theatrical, dishonest, dangerous and 'not normal behaviour'. I, on the other hand, swallowed the adoration as if it were sweet wine. The public's praise drowned out your worries, and silenced common sense.

There was an episode, in the south of the country. I had left you for a three-day congress on Data Analysis. The final morning, a few hours before returning home, I visited a local bakery called (and I do not joke) 'A Loaf of

Bread'! It had an outstanding reputation with the locals and was packed with citizens of every size, shape and age. My entry was met with a few gasps of excitement, followed by a shower of greetings and compliments from the customers within. There was praise for myself, for DIDS, the National Defence Movement and the Dear Leader. The citizens practically carried me to the front of the queue, where the baker begged to take my order before anyone else's! It was an overwhelming experience. Especially given that the totality of my life's achievements thus far did not warrant such levels of adoration. Regardless, the uninhibited love and respect expressed by these citizens gave me so much joy.

I stood at the counter, filled with a sense of greatness that raised me high above everyone else in the bakery. From such an elevated position it was clear, while I was <u>among</u> them, I was not <u>of</u> them. I was 'special'. Their joyous reaction to my presence was proof enough. So much noise! My memory now of that morning is coloured by hindsight. Had I only remembered Mother's warnings about noisy compliments. Perhaps I should have listened harder to your pleas to keep my feet on the ground. But back then, I was a hundred years younger, and my spirit so loved the praise.

Back at university, I was sometimes mocked (though more often loved) for my practice of never leaving the house without a supply of 'emergency funds'. This habit was instilled in me by Father's youngest brother. I remember him being the happiest of my three uncles. Always buzzing with energy, and always with bundles of cash that he flashed around in a manner that infuriated Father and made Mother gasp. We laughed. He lived fast and died in a cloud of scandal. Once, long ago, I asked about the banknotes. He walked over to where I stood and dropped to one knee, then he took my chin in his right hand, looked me straight in the eye, and said: 'Emergency funds. Because you never know.'

That morning, in A Loaf of Bread, I realized wearing the uniform gave me a superpower. No, I could not suddenly lift great rocks and hurl them about. But I could look at another human being and make them glow. I could enter a room and those within would become ecstatic. Officer training had instilled this in us: 'Your uniform is the voice of the NDM. Your actions tell a story to the people.' The discovery regarding the power of my uniform put me in a generous and eloquent mood. I reached into my satchel, extracted five high-denomination banknotes and placed them on the counter. The baker's confusion was amusing. I then turned to the crowd and asked them to settle down. My tongue was possessed by the spirit of the occasion.

'Mothers, fathers, brothers, sisters,' I began. 'I am honoured and humbled. The nation thrives because of citizens such as yourselves. This is an unchallengeable fact. Therefore, on behalf of the National Defence Movement, permit me to express our gratitude with a small gesture. The Division of Internal Data and Security will cover the orders of everyone here.' The citizens erupted into a joyous thunder of cheering, pats on the back, hugs, a few kisses. All so wonderful! The baker protested (mildly). She argued the money on the counter was too much, enough to pay the collective bill many times over. 'That is fine,' I said, and then declared it to be A Loaf of Bread's lucky day. Whatever amount remained after covering the bill should be seen as a tip, wrapped in the eternal appreciation of the NDM. The people were still cheering, weeping, hugging and clapping as I left. I wore a huge smile across my face and a cloak of great satisfaction over my shoulders. 'What are you?' I asked myself. 'I am a God!' Yes, I was happy with life. I felt good.

The same could not be said of our relationship with the East. Out of the blue, Eastern media began to toss around careless and aggressive allegations, claiming our people's 'shady business practices' were bleeding their country dry. This was a complete fabrication! Rather than focus on their leaders' activities, the Easterners listened to fables about our people's supposed 'natural greed and dishonesty' or about our alleged 'insufferable arrogance'. I am sorry to say, the majority of the Eastern population chose to believe this nonsense rather than think for themselves.

Their comments shocked and offended us as a nation. They rattled the Dear Leader. Why would the Eastern-ers say this? Were any of the allegations true? The EDS was asked to look into the matter. Their conclusion: the root cause of the Eastern leadership's behaviour was the impending economic (and subsequent political) collapse. The East was in deep trouble. Their citizens' previously sporadic expressions of unrest had evolved into daily occurrences that spread rapidly through the country. A pandemic of dissatisfaction loomed, and the Eastern leadership, in a state of panic, played the easiest card: scapegoat the 'other'. In this instance, we became the other. Their methods were simple and extremely effective. A number of popular commentators from the radio and papers (those with a large audience) were asked by the Eastern leadership to emphasize 'messages' that contained attacks and insults directed towards our people. The Eastern public's dissatisfaction and rage were deflected away from their leaders and refocused elsewhere. It should have taken but a sprinkle of common sense for the people to see through this ploy. However, anger, frustration and common sense are rarely ever friends.

The most influential of the Eastern commentators was a man with an extremely popular Saturday evening radio show. One evening, he proclaimed, by way of colourful melodrama, our people to be worse than cockroaches. The commentator then shared an anecdote about 'driving the sneaky, filthy cockroaches' out of his grandmother's kitchen. The vermin ate everything and left his grandmother with nothing! Had he not acted as he did, when he did, the poor woman might have starved to death. A week later, every place of trade belonging to our people in the East was attacked. Stalls, shops, kiosks were all smashed, gutted and burned. We were horrified. I remember how you sobbed. You said it could not be true. It was.

The Eastern leadership refused to condemn these acts, or express any remorse for the terror and economic loss experienced by our people. Instead, they praised the hoodlums' 'restraint' and said our people should be thankful that only shops and stalls had been destroyed. After all, the remedy for infestations of dishonest parasites was usually much worse. It broke our hearts to hear these dangerous falsehoods repeated again and again. Through our envoy in the East, the Dear Leader relayed in the strongest possible terms his disapproval of Eastern behaviour towards our nationals. As a reward, our envoy received an earful of curses. Within days, barely coherent messages and harrowing reports began to trickle in. They told of our people being driven out of Eastern towns and cities. Entire households were given no more than a few minutes to pack what they could and leave. Up to that point, I could not recall ever despising anyone. However, as I read about what was happening in the East, a hot and angry animosity towards Easterners grew within me. For the time being, this hatred served no purpose other than keeping me awake deep into the early hours. You noticed, on some of the nights you stayed over. You asked. I confessed. You suggested I find compassion and understanding for the Eastern population. 'Do you not wonder what forces have driven them to behave in this way?' By then, NDM dogma had already subverted my thinking. There was no need to wonder, I knew: the Easterners' conduct was driven by natural violent instincts. We agreed to disagree, and in the interests of our relationship I parked my dark thoughts to one side and tried to forget about them. Meanwhile, a new kind of traffic appeared at our Eastern border crossings: terrorized souls. A flood of refugees, but no strangers. These were our people, and it pained me to note their expressions carried more horror than the faces of the victims of Western aggression.

At 0930 on the morning after the last of our citizens returned, we recalled our envoy to the East and began the process of full disengagement. The border was sealed, and all new trade cancelled, with the exception of transactions finalized prior to 0800.

A brief note on the cancellation of trade with the East. One of the strategic measures implemented as a reaction to our war with the West was the creation of national reserves of essential materials. Raw materials from the East, enough to permit full manufacturing capacity for another eighteen months, were stored in hundreds of underground depots. These were spread around the country, always in areas of low population. We believed the eighteen-month margin afforded by the stockpiled material would be time enough for either the Easterners to come to their senses, or our alternative trading partners to lower their prices. Once again, the Dear Leader's vision proved correct. The Easterners believed the trade embargo to be a bluff on our part. They were wrong. Manufacturing and production continued without interruption.

Such was the state of affairs between our nations, when I arrived at the office one morning to find, in addition to my usual colleagues, three high-ranking DIDS officials. They were waiting for <u>me</u>. Highly unusual. After assuring me that all was good and well, I was thanked for my work on the National Registry, and then informed my talents were needed elsewhere. The DIDS operation was an efficient one: there was barely enough time to clear my desk and bid farewell to my colleagues. An hour later I arrived at the new Office of Easterner Observation. The name says it all. Here, we dealt with matters concerning the Easterners resident within our borders. We understood and accepted the madness in the East was driven by the scoundrels and vagabonds at the top of Eastern society. Those were desperate men and women, rotten to the core. Conditions encouraged them to lash out and blame others for their nation's misery. Generally speaking, the Easterners living with us, nurtured by the good lives they led here, were of a gentler character than their hysterical leaders. As such we did not expect them to make mischief. Yet, we saw no real harm in keeping a watchful eye on that segment of the population.

9

I believe there are moments in this life when we sense the approach of change. As if usually dormant voices within, disturbed by atmospheric vibrations or charged elements in the air, are awoken. They speak, you hear them, you feel them, but their message remains unclear. Only later, once change has altered all in its path, will you understand. Well, on <u>that</u> morning as my eyes opened, ready to greet the day, the inner voices began to chatter nervously. Their din rode with me as I cycled to NDM HQ.

I experienced the rest of the morning as a slow movement through hours weighed down by an expectant silence. Productivity levels were low. Every time the office door opened, every time one of the two telephones rang, or a pencil dropped, a bell chimed . . . a shot of adrenaline burst through our veins. We jumped and twitched and coughed. Our glances, and we could barely hold the other's eye, asked 'Do you feel it?'

The waiting ended. High-pitched rumours . . . Contact lost with the aircraft carrying the Dear Leader and a delegation of top-ranking NDM officials . . . Last known position, midway over Eastern territory. The EDS intercepted radio chatter alluding to the downing of an aircraft. Shortly thereafter we received confirmation of a crash in a remote region of the East. Identification markings matched those on the plane carrying the NDM leadership. Survivors . . . unspecified.

Such explosive information warranted urgent investigation. We managed to open a communication channel with the East and offered to assist them with the search and rescue effort. They rejected our offer, citing national sovereignty and claiming to possess the necessary expertise for such matters.

This was an unacceptable response. The matter at hand involved the fate of the entire NDM leadership. Cooperation, regardless of our diplomatic status, should be a given. We demanded immediate access to the crash site. The Easterners ignored us. They treated us like fools, obfuscating and distracting until their words made us dizzy. When we confronted them with our perception of their behaviour, the Easterners sneered at our observations while claiming ignorance. Their words were wrapped in dark shadows and dripped with lies.

It took the better part of a month to repatriate the bodies and allow us to bury our leaders with dignity. The Easterners, as if to rub salt in an open wound, sent a low-level, ragtag delegation to the Dear Leader's funeral. How they fidgeted and chatted among themselves during the burial ceremony was a disgrace! We learned that 'other matters arising' prevented the Eastern leadership from paying their final respects in person.

Our traditional national reaction to the death of a leader, regardless of political affiliation, is to enter the Two Chapters of Mourning. (The leader of our previous government was a notable exception.) The first chapter is the Month of Pain, in which all citizens in the nation are given the freedom to express such a terrible loss. We give thanks to Mother Nature for blessing us all with the capacity to feel such wretchedness. The Month of Pain begins on the night of the first full moon after a leader's burial, and lasts for twenty-eight days. The weeks following the Dear Leader's death were heavy and grey. The plants and trees, the air and the raindrops joined our mourning. A section of the nation remained frozen in collective grief, while others burned with an impotent rage.

The second chapter is the Time of Reflection: a full-moon cycle in which we recall, once again, the many ways the departed (in this case the Dear Leader) changed our lives, for better or worse. We have long since forgotten why the ancients believed it took two full-moon cycles for the collective's emotional wounds to heal. Only then, they declared, were we ready for new leadership. The Two Chapters of Mourning, like many of the old ways passed down to us by our forebears, have not aged well. I suspect our world is very different to theirs. Today is faster and more complex. We react and react and react. There is little time to reflect. I look around our tent in this doomed camp and wonder, if we had thought just a bit harder, just a bit longer, would I be here today? Who knows.

While a fair percentage of the general population used the Time of Reflection as tradition demanded, what remained of the NDM began to lash about, like the body of a decapitated snake. Nature abhors a vacuum, as does power. Vicious factional infighting quickly spread through the organization. Faction A eliminated faction B, who were removed by faction C, only to be replaced by faction D, and so on. It was a brutal and embarrassing exhibition. The quest for power brings out such ugliness of the spirit. Together with many of my fellow officers, I cringed at what was said, at what was done. We watched the contenders claw and hack their way to the top. If only they could see themselves, we thought. Eventually, the fighting stopped and the dust settled. There, standing all powerful, atop the mound of bile and machinations, was a new leader. At one o'clock on a rainy afternoon, Our Dear Leader spoke to the nation. His words jumped out of the radio speakers and into our ears. We were introduced to a new leader with a new style.

Whenever our recently deceased leader addressed the nation, he usually left us in a mood of 'thoughtful determination'. His words echoed in our minds, and encouraged us to work harder, and care more for the other. Brutal ascension aside, the Dear Leader was a man who truly loved our nation. He was at his most joyful when things changed for the better: a new hospital wing, a new school, a new factory. I met him on numerous occasions at NDM HQ, and came to see him as a leader who ruled by way of inspiration. He was a teacher whose mission, at the head of the nation, was to facilitate the elevation of others. In contrast, Our Dear Leader had a different approach. He made up for a lack of inspirational eloquence with raw power, and a unique ability to tap into the nation's mood. Our Dear Leader touched us, reached deep into our hearts, and into the very centre of our minds. He spoke, and we believed without resistance. To describe the phenomenon as mass hypnosis would be no exaggeration. We believed him when he said 'I feel your torment. Your loss is mine. The tears you shed are just as bitter as those on my face.' We believed him when he claimed 'My anger is as fierce as yours, as is my sense of betrayal.' Only a man with our best will in his heart could utter such words. We believed it when Our Dear Leader told us 'There is no need for despair. We shall have justice. We shall have justice when those who have wronged us begin to fear us. We shall have justice, people. We shall have justice! We shall have justice!' For a good minute, Our Dear Leader bellowed 'We shall – have – justice!' Again and again . . . We knew he spoke the truth. We felt it.

There were nine of us in the office. Standing, sitting, listening to the speech. As Our Dear Leader began his mantra, the room filled with an energy similar to what I had experienced during Self-Identification class.

From here, today, it occurs to me, Our Dear Leader's ability to dazzle our minds with what he <u>planned</u> to do made us forget to ask <u>how</u>! The force of his words spread across the land and removed our sadness. We began to look forward. In the meantime, Our Dear Leader allowed the nation to regain its strength and spirit before taking the next step on the road to justice. An open letter in the national papers. A well-crafted piece accusing 'certain scoundrels' of assassinating the Dear Leader and then, in the manner of cowards, lying about their deeds. As a nation, we were willing to let bygones be bygones, no matter how painful, if we received honesty in exchange. We promised there would be no retaliation or repercussions of any sort. All we asked for was the truth. The letter mentioned no names and pointed at no one in particular. Yet it was impossible to read the contents and not look east.

The official response to the letter from a furious Eastern leadership was an explosion of thunder and bombast. They ranted and raged. They declared Our Dear Leader's letter an insult of 'national proportion' and one they would never forget. The Eastern leadership's noisy focus on hurt feelings, as well as the lack of an actual denial, revealed enough. Many of us wondered how people who screamed in this manner ever managed to lead a nation. Any human being with a gram of common sense knew screaming was not an effective leadership style as it frightened away the truth. The Eastern leadership was lost in a forest of lies, without truth to guide the way. They no longer knew their left from right, nor up from down, truth from fabrication. They were blind, and afraid. Well, as we say, the frightened cat jumps in unexpected directions . . . External Data and Security reported back on the Eastern leadership's nervous desperation and increasingly erratic behaviour towards their own people. In among the chatter and vague whispers coming out of the East, the EDS detected a new willingness by their leaders to apply extreme methods in their attempt to survive. We knew the Easterners were up to something, but were unable to discover what.

10

None of us expected the terror. Markets were civilian territory. While it's true, war has destroyed many marketplaces around the world, it was always collateral damage: a poorly aimed mortar shell or bomb, the unfortunate setting for intense ground combat, but never deliberate targeting. So imagine the shock of an attack during peacetime. It was <u>not</u> warfare, this behaviour of theirs. We had never heard of, nor experienced, anything like this synchronized mindless slaughter. The nation was stunned. What should we call this merciless destruction of innocents? Blameless citizens going about their business, in the middle of the afternoon.

The three simultaneous double explosions in three marketplaces, in three cities, left too many dead. There were many hundreds of wounded, and thousands more traumatized souls. These were gangster tactics. This was <u>not</u> how nations fought. The country's eyes turned towards the Division of Internal Data and Security: 'How could this happen? Is it not your duty to keep us safe?' they asked. A number of noisy and influential voices across the media questioned whether DIDS was truly deserving of its budget. How could such a well-funded organization fail to protect the citizens? How could such tragedy be allowed to take place within our borders?

The publicly voiced accusations of waste and incompetence were painful. Our diligence and hard work had brought us to an obvious conclusion: the more we learned, the greater our understanding of how much we had yet to discover. Of course there were holes in our mesh of information. We patched them as quickly and effectively as possible, but certain clues, hints and activities escaped our attention. We tried our best, and always learned from our errors. We were not fools. All the same, the ultimate responsibility for national security lay with DIDS, and the public's anger was insatiable. Our Dear Leader sensed this and acted accordingly. Heads rolled. Our division chief and his two deputies were asked to resign. We viewed this as an unnecessary and ill-considered move. Their replacements were a trio of outsiders. The new chief immediately demanded an explanation for our incompetence. He did so by way of the radio and newspapers, and not by visiting our offices and speaking directly to us. Within DIDS, the Office of Easterner Observation took the blame.

The powers that be made it perfectly clear: we at the OEO were <u>responsible</u> for these acts of terror. Rather than sitting around in our offices, we should have been out there, preventing such ideas from developing into plots and subsequent horror. We were a national disgrace. An embarrassment to the Division of Internal Data and Security, an embarrassment to the National Defence Movement, and currently unmentionable to Our Dear Leader. The list of our wrongs was enough to have the Office of Easterner Observation disbanded with immediate effect. Fortunately, the NDM was not a cruel organization, and the OEO was given two weeks to save itself by identifying and capturing those responsible. With this threat ringing in our ears, the OEO staff created new definitions for focus, analysis and overtime.

We had very little information to work with. The timing of the three market bombings suggested they were carefully planned acts. The culprits remained invisible, though we strongly suspected Eastern involvement. As if in harmony with our increasingly fraught relationship with the East, we noted increased agitation among certain groups of Easterners. However, a motive for the bombing, beyond careless destruction of life, remained unclear. Who had devised such a wicked plot? Where had the planning taken place? These were questions beyond the scope of our data. We had no idea where to begin, and therefore chose to begin with <u>everything</u>.

The OEO sent out urgent requests to all our eyes and ears on the ground for reports of any memorable activities noticed during the weeks and days leading up to the bombings. It need not be criminal behaviour. We asked for anything that had made someone look twice, or lingered in their minds longer than usual. Fate came to our rescue. An informant reported back. An hour before the bombings, she and a few friends were having lunch on the terrace of a popular establishment in the west of the city. I knew the place by name, though had never visited. It was run by a couple of Eastern descent, and our records had it down as a favourite watering hole for artists, musicians and literary types, of all ages and nationalities.

During a lull in the afternoon conversation, our informant overheard a child ask his mother if two men had a fever: why else would they wear heavy coats on such a hot afternoon? Our informant turned and recognized the subjects of the conversation. The two men, clad in oversized and heavily padded coats, had not been wearing those garments thirty minutes earlier, when they arrived at the establishment and walked inside. Our informant remembered the men's faces: 'As if they were in a trance,' she said. 'And their eyes, they were empty.' At the time, our informant believed the two men were simply another pair of oddly dressed Easterners.

Further analysis of informants' reports from the three affected cities revealed eleven unique references of men wearing unseasonably heavy coats and walking towards or in the vicinity of the markets, prior to the bomb attacks. Was there a relationship between the watering hole and the stricken market twenty minutes away? Given the urgency of the situation (remember, the OEO was fighting for its survival), we took risks where we had once acted with caution. At two thirty in the morning, thirteen hours after receiving the new information, I looked around at my tired colleagues. The strong coffee, rather than helping, had turned against us: it stimulated our ability not to think in a clear manner, and nothing else. We were desperate. Empty. Unable to decide how best to proceed. A wrong move, and those we sought might escape. Our paralysis was caused by an inability to understand the thinking of those behind the bombings. The office clock chimed the half-hour. The gleeful 'ding' was accompanied by a flash of memory from officer training: 'Defeat and indecision are the best of friends.' My penchant for dithering was gone by the time I completed officer training. I knew what to do. Rather than take time to observe the suspect establishment in the west of the city, we raided it the following evening.

I am amused at how often we miss what stands right in front of our noses. The art, music and poetry was a distraction. Behind a false wall in the basement, we discovered a workshop. Tools, maps, knives, guns, ammunition and a whole range of items that challenged the knowledge of our technical staff. Of great interest was an area dedicated to inserting explosives inside everyday objects: coats, children's dolls, radios. I saw this with my own eyes. Such behaviour was unheard of, and I firmly believed at the time the hidden workshop to be the Devil's domain.

Within a week, five of the market-bombing masterminds were in our custody. Utilizing the wide variety of data extraction tools and methods at our disposal, we soon discovered connections between our five captives and certain influential individuals in the East. We noted how our guests' minds were filled with an unfortunate and incomplete view of the world. In their version, the problems in the East were a direct result of Our Dear Leader's spiteful actions. No mention was made of the role played by the corrupt Eastern leadership. When we challenged their beliefs with facts, the five accused us of concocting lies and other conspiracies. Internally, I sneered at the inability of their minds to see the brightly illuminated truth, even when held up on a platter right before their eyes! I saw these people as wicked, ignorant souls, lacking the intelligence to separate right from wrong. After all, what in Heaven's name was right about blowing up market-going innocents? I now have a much better understanding of such behaviour. Those five were not stupid, they were simply too busy <u>acting</u> to <u>think</u> about their actions. At the time, we noted their attitude but found it of secondary importance to the fact we finally had information to work with.

During the creation of the EDS and DIDS, care was taken to accommodate the fact that where there are people, there are egos . . . The sense of competition was kept to a minimum, and the boundaries between our divisions were designed to mimic the nation's porous borders.

The free flow of data traffic was essential for complete national security coverage. The inter-divisional cooperation on the market bombings project was outstanding, and our five captive masterminds were exceptionally helpful. They provided a list of twenty-seven new candidates for investigation. Those twenty-seven, in turn, gave us access to another hundred and thirty-three. Those were days of long hours and night-time work: scouring, cross-checking, extracting.

Most of the Eastern candidates we brought in were more than happy to help with our inquiries. Some, perhaps inspired by popular literature and film, chose the path of dogged heroism. Yet they too eventually came to their senses and realized it was better for all when they cooperated. An unfortunate few, due to a stubborn refusal to assist in a positive manner, found themselves in a condition that was of no use to us, or anyone else.

With renewed dedication and intensified focus, we spent the next five weeks identifying and subsequently destroying every node on the subversive Eastern terror network that threatened our nation's well-being. The speed and efficiency of our endeavours impressed the top layers of the NDM, all the way up to Our Dear Leader.

The Office of Eastern Observation was safe for now. We also heard, though this was never confirmed, our work had some influence on the content and tone of his next speech.

Our Dear Leader's voice filled the radio waves as he addressed the Easterners living among us: 'We welcomed you into our home as mothers, fathers, brothers, sisters, daughters and sons.' We heard the flames of rage as they spat and crackled around his words. 'We welcomed you as new members of our family and, because it is our nature to do so, we trusted you as we trust ourselves. We granted your wishes to build the houses of worship your culture requires. We gave you the freedom to think as you please. For countless seasons you have lived with us, in harmony, in prosperity. Why this? Why mimic the barbarous antics of your country's leadership?' Our Dear Leader declared himself to be an understanding man, who knew most Easterners were just as horrified by the market bombings as any other right-thinking beings. However, the slaughter had been planned and carried out in the Easterners' name. They had stood by and watched as a poisonous few of their people brought the malevolent scheme to life. No voices were raised in disagreement, and no attempt was made to warn us, their hosts, of the impending chaos and bloodshed. 'Such a pity,' Our Dear Leader said. 'Such disregard for our kindness and accommodation. Well, we have a message for those of you who choose to repay our generous hospitality with murder . . . We will find you. Do you hear that, Easties? Run far, hide low, do whatever you like. We will track and hunt you, drag you out from your filthy lairs, and bring you to face the consequences of your actions!'

'Easties' was a term approved and inserted into Our Dear Leader's speech by a special team within NDM Messaging and Public Relations that was focused on Easterners. Not a day went by during my time with the OEO without a member of that team popping into our office to ask for the latest summary of Easterner-relevant information, or to seek further clarification of one or another Easterner trait. Within the OEO we referred to Easterners as 'Easties'. This was out of convenience (one less syllable) rather than malice. The team from Messaging and Public Relations who, by the way, could transform a fresh drop of rain into acid, picked up on 'Eastie'. They liked it and passed it on to Our Dear Leader, who used it in his speech. The term stuck. From that day on, the resident Easterners became Easties, the enemy within.

11

One of the new measures relating to control of the Easties living among us was the Oath. A straightforward Oath
of Allegiance to the nation and Our Dear Leader. What
Easties thought, or how they behaved outside of our borders, was their own business. However, due to the actions
of their fellow countryfolk, we were left with no choice
but to clarify what was expected of guests in our land.
The Oath was an agreement to abide by a set list of what
Easties were and were not permitted to do. It might help
to remember, these reduced freedoms existed as a result
of Eastie behaviour. We would rather have done without
them, but circumstances . . .

We understood that, for many Easties, taking the Oath
was a purely pragmatic act: it allowed them to get on
with their lives, and as far as we were concerned, that was
fine. Those who took the Oath usually had no interest
in politics or conspiracies. We knew this because we, at
the OEO, watched them. The secondary purpose of the
Oath was to identify members of a category we called the

Potentially Disruptive Eastie (PDE). Refusal to take the Oath signalled a stubbornness of character, and with it an aptitude for causing trouble. Once identified and marked accordingly, those in the PDE category were placed on the Action Pending Register (APR).

I tell you, the NDM were masters of lyrical chicanery: Action Pending was nothing more than a sugar coating applied to 'marked for punishment'. Again the Easties brought trouble upon themselves. It would not reflect well on the nation, or Our Dear Leader, if those Easties who refused to pledge allegiance walked free and unsanctioned. It was tantamount to a slap in the face! Were Easties allowed to insult Our Dear Leader and go free, what would be next? Hurling rotten fruit and rocks at the man? Violence? The Action Pending punishment was savage in how it always struck the hapless Eastie where it hurt most.

Another of the available methods of Eastie control was through the issuance of residency permits. A mere formality for those who had taken the Oath, the residency permit allowed Easties to reside in, or own property within our borders, so long as they paid the respective charges and taxes in full and on time. Potentially Disruptive Easties on the APR were deemed too unstable for permanent residency. As such, their permit requests were denied. The law being as it was, any Eastie without a residency permit was naturally given Unlawful Resident (UR) status. The consequence of UR status was an official Declaration of Illegality (DI). The sanctions for a DI included immediate forfeiture of all assets (excepting personal items able to be carried without mechanical assistance) and deportation to the land of ancestral origin.

Running parallel to these adjustments was an Eastie 'derecognition' campaign, managed by NDM Messaging and Public Relations. The aim was to highlight the 'natural, cultural and moral differences' between ourselves and our Eastie guests. Recent exposure to the violent facets of Eastie behaviour helped it along. The campaign also coincided with a shift in the nation's mood. Our hearts and minds were filled with a growing euphoria, an ecstasy conjured up by Our Dear Leader's words. Goodness knows how many times we passed wild-eyed citizens in the streets chanting, out loud, Our Dear Leader's phrases. Quoting his words!

I remember the bizarre incident in the library on that wet afternoon. You and I, together with thirty or so others, had run inside to take shelter from an unexpected rainstorm. In the foyer was an exhibition of portraits of Our Dear Leader. The artists were children, and it was clear they viewed Our Dear Leader as a God-like being. The collection of youthful artistic expression and adoration dizzied our minds. But that was nothing compared to the spontaneous outburst from almost everyone in the space. One moment there was the semi-excited hubbub of those who have just escaped a downpour, the next, an explosion of wild chanting of praise for Our Dear Leader. I found it amusing, you found it worrisome.

Our Dear Leader was very good with words. He weighed, arranged and fed them to us. The nation swallowed without resistance. Although, through the filters of time and circumstance, I realize just how much of what came out of his mouth was no more than well-dressed nonsense. That said, the man's execution was sublime. The force with which he delivered his loud assertions allowed us to ignore their hollow ring. Back then, there was a belief, a highly charged nationwide state of mind, that we, led by Our Dear Leader, were on the verge of greatness. The majority of us sensed the time had come to write a new chapter into the history books.

Accompanying the euphoria was a growing darkness. It manifested in how we vocalized our mistrust and dislike of Easties. Commentary about Easties inserted itself into daily conversation, none of it complimentary. Radio and theatre comics made Easties the target of many a joke. Where wit and surprise had once been used to entertain us, the public now took delight in the vicious skewering of Eastie characteristics. Those comics were brutal, extremely funny, and every one of them was pushed forward and promoted by NDM Messaging and Public Relations. How many shows did I see? Three, four? I sit here and recall how I laughed. Belly in agony, cheek muscles aching, tears streaming. You fidgeted through the first show: not really your kind of entertainment . . .

The jokes that had the nation splitting its sides were just the beginning: our first steps down the path of derecognition, and, eventually, complete dehumanization of the Easties. Had we known, would we have laughed so hard, or stopped and changed direction? Who knows. As I recall, we, as a nation, thoroughly enjoyed the humiliation of the Easties. Why this bigoted vulgarity made so many of us feel so good, I cannot say.

The radio and newspapers were next to join in. Theirs

was a humourless contribution. An endless series of articles, news items and commentary focused on Eastie misbehaviour. Eastie misappropriations of funds, Eastie molestation of grandmothers, Eastie cartel forming, Eastie membership of criminal organizations, attempted subversion, violent beliefs. No actual evidence of Eastie wrongdoing was ever revealed, only exceptionally well-dressed innuendo and vague allegations presented as fact. Quack scientists passed comment in the broadsheets or on air. They told us Easties lacked the higher levels of morality found in other civilized beings. Easties had a non-complex culture. Easties had naturally limited intellectual capacity. Eastie language was too primitive to contain nuance. The majority of the nation, myself included, swallowed this 'science' as if it were nourishment.

The media enhanced their reporting of Eastie activities with sensational eyewitness accounts of those who had been insulted, double-crossed or scandalized. There were heartbreaking tales of our children trying to play in public parks, only to be terrified and chased away by rough-mannered Eastie offspring. Behind the noise, I heard the sound of NDM Messaging and Public Relations, and behind that, the voice of Our Dear Leader.

As the anti-Eastie sentiments spread across the land, my work at the OEO began to lose its shine. I spent most of my time as an NDM officer inside an office, performing a routine series of actions over and over again. The only escape from those walls, windows and perfectly arranged desks were a few mandatory combat courses. I loved them, even though they fed my annoyance at having missed action during our fight with the Westerners. I began to choke. I needed to breathe, to run and shout.

A few months prior to the Dear Leader's assassination, a thirteen-strong DIDS team was assigned to the NDM Ministry of Housing and Justice. The plan was to provide consultation and training for ministry officials on the matters of data extraction, collation and analysis. The DIDS team would depart once ministerial levels of information competence were attained. The ascension of Our Dear Leader adjusted these plans. The DIDS section was absorbed by the Ministry of Housing and Justice and transformed into the Property Integrity Office (PIO). The PIO's remit was the management of all state properties. Various units within the PIO were given specific areas of specialization: parks, bridges, public buildings, housing, inspection, renovation, etc.

During the development of the National Registry, I had liaised with and come to know a number of people in the Ministry of Housing and Justice who currently operated within the PIO. We remained in touch: a beer here, a coffee there. During an evening drink with my PIO friends, I received a tip about a recruitment drive for the new Data and Security action teams within the PIO. The creation of these teams was a natural consequence of the increasing need for DIDS to carry out practical field work. And the teams were <u>not</u> office bound. The thought of operating outside of a building was sweet music to my soul! I applied and was accepted immediately: those higher up fast-tracked my transfer to the PIO. My excellent service record being a major factor in their considerations. I received two months of intensive training, which involved absorbing huge chunks of National Law. On completion, I moved up a rank and was given command of an action team: a PIO Site Inspection Unit (SIU).

The minister in charge declared the action teams to be the Ministry of Data and Security's surgical instruments, and the Potentially Disruptive Easties, having resisted the prescribed ointment of the Oath, the diseased flesh in need of removal.

My SIU was tasked with the preparation of properties for renovation. It does not take complex science to understand it is impossible to renovate a property and return it to a suitable 'living' condition when inhabited by unlawful residents. Our task began with the extraction of occupants. The first stage in this process was an Appropriation Order (AO) for the property to be renovated. As the AO made its way through the chambers of the Ministry of Housing and Justice to my SIU, it was joined by Unlawful Residency Status documents and official Declaration(s) of Illegality. What eventually arrived was a package of documents filled with complicated texts.

The extraction process began when we arrived at the site in need of inspection and presented the occupants with the official DI. My approach was to do so while quoting from the sections of National Law governing low moral standards, antisocial, subversive, potentially anti-national behaviour, and the consequences thereof. By the way, the information gleaned from the National Registry allowed for extremely effective targeting of Potentially

Disruptive Easties. We encouraged the occupant representative receiving the official DI to sign where necessary on the papers and accept the transfer of assets (residential and otherwise) to the NDM Ministry of Housing and Justice. With that done, I then made clear to the former occupants their Unlawful Resident status required them to leave the country within forty-eight hours. The Unlawful Resident Transfer Squads, who accompanied our SIU, would provide further assistance. We shuttered the property and then set off to our next inspection.

Site Inspections were not always smooth, straightforward affairs. The Easties employed, understandably, a wide range of delaying tactics. Everything from chaining themselves to immovable items, to feigning ill health or encouraging friendly neighbours to create all manner of peripheral distractions. We accepted these delays as an unfortunate component of the business. Occasionally, our arrival for a Site Inspection motivated occupants to discover a new, sudden and dramatic enthusiasm to take the Oath. They offered to do so right then and there, and were always disappointed, at times shocked, to learn our SIU lacked the authority to grant such requests. We understood how such sudden changes in circumstance would challenge anyone's spirits, and so, without fail, we waited with great patience as the forlorn Easties vacated the property.

The effects of the change in national mood and direction eventually made their way down to the PIO Site Inspection Units. We received a directive announcing a number of adjustments to our inspection methods. A growing number of Easties living among us had begun renouncing their Oaths. These acts of renunciation were often public affairs that included the burning of Oath of Allegiance certificates and other examples of Eastie thuggery. They claimed their barbaric conduct was no more than an expression of solidarity with extracted family, friends, and so on. Recent studies by prominent NDM sociologists had revealed the Easties' lack of capacity for natural honesty. Evidence could be seen in the ease with which these people tossed aside sworn Oaths. Of course these Easties were placed on the APR.

The escalating Eastie agitation had been duly noted, and an adequate response formulated. The new directive increased the number of daily Site Inspections by a factor of three. At the same time it decreased our tolerance for delays. We were requested to keep logistical hold-ups to an absolute minimum by 'utilizing all available resources and methods in the removal of hindrances'.

As mentioned earlier, the Easties were a wonderfully creative lot when it came to inventing excuses not to leave illegally appropriated ministry property. For example, they would argue back and forth forever about what gave us the right to act as we did. They demanded proof that our official documents had <u>actually</u> come from the Ministry of Housing and Justice. Can you imagine? Some even challenged us to prove how not signing an Oath automatically signified disdain for Our Dear Leader. Others spoke at length about the grandfathers, great uncles and aunts who built the properties they illegally occupied, throwing in the occasional claims of barehanded construction. As if we would bother our heads with such information! Prior to the new directive, our approach to occupant extraction had been non-physical, respectful and one of gentle persuasion. It could take anything up to six hours to fully vacate a property. Most of that time was consumed by debate.

Our 'new style' began with a reduction in patience. Where we had once tutted and sighed, while drumming our fingers against thighs, we now pushed and dragged. Occasionally, though only ever when the situation demanded, there might be need for a motivational slap or a punch or kick. Had time not been of the essence, I would have instructed the men to exercise restraint. However, proceedings needed to keep moving at a reasonable pace.

Another request listed in the directive was for the Site Inspection Units to share their on-site experiences. These reports and anecdotes were compiled into a reference library of extraction techniques. We learned what methods worked best, and when and how to employ them.

I have learned there are mad beasts inside us all. Under normal circumstances, these inner monsters never get the chance to come out and play. Our behaviour is prevented from straying beyond acceptable moral boundaries by our National Laws. Well, you know how we men love to push and smash through our barriers? Those five words, 'all available resources and methods', freed the beasts within us. The pushing and slapping, the kicking and prodding, evolved into beating and bludgeoning. In our view, the Easties brought this treatment upon themselves with their unnecessary attachment to material goods (including property) and stubborn refusal to accept the letter of our laws. Every one of the Unlawful Residents extracted from the appropriated properties had been given ample opportunity to express their respect for Our Dear Leader and the nation. They refused, and chose instead to make trouble.

From my current position, I see events from a different perspective. To drag people out of their homes and expect no resistance was sheer madness. Imagine yourself in a similar situation. I would certainly not leave politely. Perhaps we wished for the Easties to kick up a fuss and make trouble. Such behaviour then gave us justification to act as we did.

12

One evening, with multiple units involved in a large-scale Site Inspection, I witnessed two extraction disputes resolved with a bullet. The location, a high-rise complex in Southside. The population was predominantly Eastie, and the area a known hotbed of radical thought and opinion. It was home to many Potentially Disruptive Easties. A huge, raging Eastie refused to accept his UR status, and would not leave the property. He bellowed and cursed and stretched the patience of the officer in charge until it snapped. I was close enough to see an expression of surprise light up the Eastie brute's face before he collapsed to the ground. The man had been given an opportunity to leave quietly, and refused. Two floors below, a grey-haired fellow, carrying too many kilos of flesh, charged an SIU soldier with a bread knife. There was no need for a warning. His wife howled, the family dog barked as if it had lost its mind. The officer in charge ordered one of the men to attend to the baying hound. In both instances, I noted the surrounding reactions, especially the faces of the officers in charge. They remained calm, and I thought of a laboratory assistant mounting an insect onto a card.

Of course these incidents rattled my nerves, nausea attacked my guts and throat, but I hid this from the world around me. It was the wise thing to do. Many questions ran through my head as I watched the killings. 'Is this the right way to act?' or 'Why do you pretend to feel nothing?' or 'What are you doing here?' were not among them. Instead, my primary queries were about the ability and speed with which I could push the horror to one side and gather myself together. It took but a matter of seconds. I recited the mantra 'What are you?' 'I am a God!', straightened my back, and then adjusted to our new way of doing business with ease. Click. Just like that. 'All available resources and methods . . .'

There is one Site Inspection, a sticky memory, I would very much like to forget. I cannot. It was morning, and I led eight men to a neighbourhood north-west of Little River. As a child, I had occasionally passed through the area and never ceased to be impressed by the magnificent, sprawling villas. The homes here were glorious. They exuded wealth, power and comfort. With no more than the family home and those of my friends and relatives as reference,

I imagined that the families living in the villas must have tens of children. Why else live in a house that size?

We travelled together with an Unlawful Resident Transfer Squad. This was standard for such trips. There was also a Process Inspector, who would spend the day with our unit, monitoring activities and making notes. Occasionally there was a disconnect between methods thought up in the office and what took place on the ground. Process Inspectors located these fissures and prescribed solutions for areas in need of improvement. The PI's comments were never judgemental. They were usually helpful. It was our fifth Site Inspection with a PI in attendance, we were now used to their presence and went about our business as usual. I hoped, by the end of the day, to show our PI outstanding examples of Site Inspection practices.

Thus far, I had never been directly involved in the violence. This had nothing to do with shirking responsibilities, discomfort or fear of dirtying my hands. It happened that the men under my command were a proactive and enthusiastic lot, who enjoyed their work. I saw no reason to get in the way. My style was to stand back, oversee proceedings, and issue guidance when necessary.

We had an official Declaration of Illegality for the residents of No. 17. Our records had them down as a powerful Eastie trading family. Half of their business was conducted in our land, the rest in the East. Our records also told us that three of their five primary trading partners had links to radical elements within the Eastern power structure. This alone was not enough to place them under suspicion. However, in addition to the family refusing to sign the Oath, we had recordings of both parents demeaning the policies of the NDM, and witnesses to them publicly criticizing the stewardship of Our Dear Leader. Given these facts, even the most lenient Ministry of Housing and Justice officials would have no choice but to see the family for what they were: Potentially Disruptive Easties. Immediate Unlawful Resident status!

The weather was exceptionally bright. No. 17 was partially hidden from the road by a tall, precision-trimmed hedge and rows of slender trees. The route from the gate to the property's front door was breathtaking. We passed through a beautifully landscaped garden, where armies of flowers guarded a series of rolling slopes. There was a large pond with five wooden benches of superior quality.

At its centre was a fountain where three intertwined frogs, frozen in mid-leap, spewed thin jets of water from their open mouths. The glistening, twisting stream rose a good few metres into the air before falling back into the pond with musical splashes.

The Eastie family opened the door when we rang the bell. This kept us in a good mood. You would not believe the number of times we arrived for inspection only to have occupants pretend not to be home. The results were always the same: broken front doors. The occupants of No. 17 were an Eastie mother and her four offspring aged, I would say, between seventeen and twenty-five years: three males and a female. The father was away on business, which was no bother. In the husband's absence, the Ministry of Housing and Justice granted the wife full authority to sign the necessary documents. The signature was of course optional. We understood how the nerve-jangling nature of our inspections might make an Eastie struggle to put pen to paper. We made allowances for such conditions and also accepted thumbprints.

I immediately sent four men off to look around the property, and then offered the mother a few minutes to make her decision to sign, or not. In truth, her choice had no effect on our business. The arrival of a Site Inspection Unit at a location was as clear an indication as any that the Ministry of Housing and Justice had issued the occupants with official Declarations of Illegality. Why else would we be there?

The family had a typical reaction: shock and disbelief, followed by plenty of fumbling and muttering. This eventually gave way to acceptance of the situation. The mother, the female offspring and the eldest male hastily, and commendably, steadied their nerves. The mother explained that the absent husband would clear up any misunderstandings the instant he returned. She asked if we could please wait another three days. I corrected the mother on the matter of misunderstandings: there were none. As for the requested delay, our unit lacked the authority to adjust procedural schedules at such short notice. The two youngest males did not react well to the news, and began to express a noisy, quite irritating panic. The younger of the two commenced a hysterical sobbing. It was a terrible sound, and fortunately for all of our ears, the mother took pity. She pulled him into her arms, gave comfort and calmed him down.

As for the property itself, I had only ever seen inside

such places in the cinema, and on the pages of Mother's magazines. Had I not been on official business, my mouth might have dropped open at the sight of the finery adorning the entrance hall. I had grown up with an awareness of Easties, though my interactions with them were rare, always distant but polite. A few lived in my neighbourhood, some attended my school, university. That said, I never had Eastie friends or found a reason to seek out their company. There was no animosity or ill feeling of any kind. We had no contact because we were fundamentally different kinds of human beings. I had no issues with difference and variety, as they brought colour and inspiration into our world. I did, however, like the rest of the nation, have difficulty when the behaviour and activities of our guests had a negative impact on the lives of the hosts. The lack of contact also meant I had never seen the interior of an Eastie house. It was a pleasantly surprising experience.

One of my first impressions was the height of the ceiling, and the ingenious use of wood to create frames supporting the walls and floors. The door handles, light switches, bannister adornments, etc. were patterned with intricate sequences of ovals and circles. They appeared to be in constant motion, and made me dizzy.

The architect's remit must have included bringing as much light as possible into the house. Sunbeams on this beautiful morning found their way into most rooms in the house. The rooms themselves were extraordinary and they too had a hypnotic effect on the senses. I was forced to station one of the men outside the front gate as it became impossible to convince him that the property was not possessed with Eastie magic. I understood the man's point of view: every room in the house was blessed with its own distinct identity. Crossing the threshold from one room to another was like moving between worlds.

One room in particular held my attention. On the second floor, on the north side of the house, was a library. The walls were covered in bookshelves, filled to an unsafe degree with books. There was little furniture in the room. At the south end stood a magnificently constructed wooden lectern. The antique edition resting on its adjustable top was a book I had read about, but never seen with my own eyes. Turning the pages was a humbling experience. At the north end of the library, a pair of chairs sat in conversation close to the large window. And the view! A magnificent garden park rolled gently downhill towards a lake. I saw a wooden pier, a red boathouse, a variety of trees, arrangements of perfectly trimmed hedges dancing with benches, statues . . . Beyond the lake was a forest, dense and mysterious. I could easily have spent the rest of the day sitting in one of the chairs, reading, gazing out of the window for a while, before reading some more. But duty called.

Another item of note: on entering the house, our nostrils were met by a delicious aroma. Not one I recognized, other than perhaps the faint echo of cinnamon. The sheer culinary goodness infused in that fragrance made it impossible for the men not to start blinking and licking their lips. I wondered what the Process Inspector made of it. I followed the sweet smell to the kitchen and discovered a stew simmering away in a huge pan. There was enough to feed a squad of hungry men. 'Expecting guests?' I asked the eldest male, who shadowed me during my ground-floor inspection. He replied with a sullen grunt that said nothing. There was a faint glint of defiance in his eyes.

I had never seen so much vegetation inside a home. While the landscaped interior garden at NDM HQ was impressive, the variety and arrangement of greenery at No. 17 left me speechless. Plants everywhere. They had colonized half the interior of the house! It had more in common with a botanical garden than with a residence. Perhaps turning the insides of one's home into a forest was an Eastie custom. If so, it was a fine tradition. There was a soothing quality to the ubiquitous flora.

The family had a fondness for portraits, though not of themselves. Every wall on the ground floor, with the exception of those in the kitchen, had at least two framed portraits. The faces looked out at the world without comment, leaving the impression of being stared at by ghosts. A few were painted in styles I recognized from museum visits, the rest were alien, though beautiful and hypnotically interesting. While I was inspecting one particular portrait, in an attempt to understand how it could affect my head as it did, the men returned with the preliminary 'reports' of their Site Inspections. We were ready.

Three minutes later, I addressed the family members in the entrance hall. I handed the mother the necessary papers and indicated where we required her signature, or thumbprint. She accepted the documents and then, to our surprise, began to sing out loud. I did not understand the words, yet I felt the great sadness they carried. Her voice was so beautiful I could not order her to stop. To do so felt criminal. At no point during her recital did the mother make eye contact with me or any of the men. The mother finished the song, and then signed. The young female's eyes spat fire.

I took the signed copies of the document from the mother, folded one copy, placed it in an official envelope, and then handed that to the young female. By this time, the mother had returned to comforting her youngest. His sniffling and quaking annoyed me intensely, as it compelled me to share in his fear. I needed him out of my sight.

Under the accelerated inspection programme, illegal occupants received fifteen minutes in which to vacate the premises with whatever they could carry. On the matter of carrying, I was surprised at how many Easties overestimated their strength, and to such a large degree. The afternoon before the inspection at No. 17, I witnessed a middle-aged man attempt to move his mother's grand piano single-handed! We tried our best not to laugh. We were, after all, in the middle of official business . . .

That morning at No. 17, rather than offer the usual fifteen minutes, I took into account the tasteful elegance of the property, and gave the family half an hour to remove themselves from the premises. I explained my reasoning to the Process Inspector. As expected, she neither agreed nor disagreed with me. In truth, there was another reason for the time extension: it provided an opportunity for another quick visit to the family's library.

Twenty-three minutes later, the family, minus the mother, stood in the entrance hall. In their hands, wrapped across shoulders, and strapped onto their backs were suitcases, bags and articles of clothing. The eldest male wore a lampshade on his head. Quite a sight. I remember the confusion written across the two younger males' faces.

My next move was to select a cigarette from the pack in my breast pocket and light up, all the while observing the young Easties with an affected air of total disinterest. I am sure you would laugh at this, but you knew, just as I did, my whole smoking business was nothing but show. I smoked when bored during parties. I stood and posed, cigarette in hand, with members of the public who asked (always with deference) to have a photograph taken standing next to me. Of course I smoked on the job. One segment of our Site Inspection training focused on the value of what they termed 'non-vocal' communication. Within this module was a lesson on 'Situational Attitude', where we were taught how best to express the three Ds: Disdain, Disgust and Disinterest. We learned which of the Ds worked best, and under what circumstances. I discovered the sight of me casually puffing away while those around me shivered in terror, anger and panic introduced a certain panache. Sad to say, the moment was soured by the mother's absence. I dispatched three men to discover the cause of the delay. They returned a minute later requesting my presence upstairs.

I found the mother in the first-floor master bedroom, kneeling beside a dresser. In this room-world, the ovals and circles found on the fittings around the house were given carte blanche. Lights, mirrors and wallpaper patterns were all oval in form, as was the bed, with an oval mattress to match. The mother's attachment to the dresser was understandable. It was a magnificent piece of furniture, and I truly hope whoever owns it today does so with appreciation.

The mother knelt and whispered. It might have been in prayer, or a goodbye to an old friend. Her lips moved, tears dripped from her cheeks onto the parquet floor. Touching. But we did not have the time for Eastie theatrics. I had two men carry her downstairs, while another took care of her luggage.

The young Easties turned their mother's arrival into a highly emotional moment. Moaning, wailing, plenty of tears. Excessive and unnecessary. The mother had been upstairs for only a few minutes longer than everyone else, <u>not</u> recently pardoned while on the way to meet the hangman's noose. At the time, I believed it was a display of the volatile emotions that distinguished a simpler, more primitive being. It was a very sad scene. By reflex, without thinking (perhaps you will have difficulty understanding such a gesture, given the circumstances), I stepped forward and laid my hand on the mother's right shoulder. It was meant as an act of comfort. The mother responded by spinning around and snarling like a wild creature. This was our first eye contact since the Site Inspection Unit's arrival, and I tell you, it took much of my resolve not to wither. Such was the force of her glare.

The mother's expression was frosty and laced with disgust. 'Let me tell you,' she began. 'This uniform cannot hide what you do. It cannot hide the fact that apart from being a thug and a thief, you are nothing!' She concluded her statement by stepping forward and spitting in my face. I heard the slow bubbling noises made by her saliva as it dripped down my right cheek.

13

Sometimes life is much too fast. We act, and cannot remember why. I have searched for a reason to explain my conduct at No. 17, but the riddle remains unsolved. There is only the drawn-out recollection of events.

The room fell silent, a mad ringing erupted between my ears. Was the tingle of embarrassment that moved from one patch of my skin to another visible to everyone else? Pride had just been punctured in public and so Ego stepped in and demanded revenge. As I wiped my face clean with a handkerchief, the youngest male tried to suppress a giggle. He failed. Was it the thoroughly annoying squeak, or the look on his face? I cannot say. Whatever the case, a fury rose up from my toes, through my legs, my torso, and entered my heart.

This memory business can be strange. The version of events at No. 17 that currently fills my mind is not quite as I once recalled it. The setting, the players, the actions remain the same. However, now my memories are awash with details I had either avoided, forgotten or missed.

Do our minds record everything but keep it locked away somewhere safe until the time is right? The approach of our end has freed these memories.

The hall was so quiet I heard the sound of my handkerchief landing on the floor. In my head, a chorus of 'What are you?' 'I am a God!' and the edict from NDM officer training: 'It is of vital importance that the officer of the National Defence Movement remains in control, and separates necessary action from the banality of emotion.'

Here today, those words ring hollow as the shiny suit worn by a charlatan while he impresses a gullible subject. What, in Heaven's name, is 'banality of emotion'? I tell you from personal experience, a life disconnected from feeling is a terrible form of existence.

In the bright silence at No. 17, I became acutely aware of the men: watching, waiting. The Process Inspector looked on and took notes. The mother's stare projected hate and disgust. The young female's eyes threw fire. The eldest male offspring twitched and appeared nervous. The second to youngest stared at his feet. The last, the little one, wore a smirk and a look in his eyes that did not rest kindly with me.

I suppressed an urge to rage and scream at the mother.

How I would have loved to shout at the top of my voice, as a God, and demand an explanation for such vulgarity. I would ask how spitting in my face would resolve her grievances with the Ministry of Housing and Justice. However, such an outburst would have been very low in dignity. I held my tongue.

I would much rather not tar a whole people with a single brush. However, my experience commanding an SIU had shown there were no limits to the aggression expressed by Easties as we extracted them from appropriated properties. Generally speaking, they were barbaric and lacked any form of self-control. No amount of finery or wealth could disguise an Eastie's true character. Case in point: the mother and her venomous spitting. Although her actions were driven by genetic composition and, on a certain level, no fault of her own, it would have been better for all if she had remained in control of these tendencies. On that sunny morning, I saw no connection between the Easties' aggression and our Site Inspection Units tossing them out of their homes. I saw in the mother nothing but another wild, uncivilized being.

The spittle itself, while unpleasant, was harmless enough. The problem lay in the contempt behind the mother's actions. Such behaviour was, as I believed at the time, an insult to myself and my uniform, to the nation, and to Our Dear Leader. My rank and position compelled me to make a point about this matter. My eyes came to rest on the youngest of the mother's offspring. The manner in which she comforted him earlier on marked him out as her favourite. My decision spanned an age. There was a voice. Front-left of mind. An earnest, whispered caution: 'He is just a boy!'

The youngest stood before me. Quivering lips blocked his words. There was a frightened animal noise, a sound that lived between a cry and a groan. 'He is just a boy!' Again <u>that</u> voice. Followed by a quiet moment, and then a response, a loud and righteous chorus from the opposite side of my mind: 'What are you?' My body answered . . .

My arm rose slowly until the barrel of the pistol, held in my hand, pointed towards the young one's nose. His eyes became wide-open pools, and unhindered dread rippled the surface. I watched the Eastie's expression transform into terrified understanding about his very near future. Tears began a slow, downward crawl over his cheeks.

'He is just a boy!' That voice again, though now far away and barely audible, shouted into submission by the mighty chorus. 'What are you?' 'I am the answer.' 'I am Authority. I will decide because I am a God.'

I heard the mother's intake of breath. A powerful, endless hiss. A decision made. The trigger accepted my finger's pull. A click. A flash. A young life reached the end of its journey. One last whisper. 'He was just a boy.'

There were screams. All members of the Eastie family screamed. The offspring, the mother. My eyes, and I know this cannot be so, watched the mother's screams create a thousand cracks across her skin. Her eyes begged me to tell her it was a lie. I remember thinking about my uniform, the nation, Our Dear Leader and the Greater Glory. The mother crumbled and collapsed in a heap over her young offspring's body. It was as if her insides and outsides had turned to salt. That was my doing. This was my work.

At that same instant, I was overcome by a terrible sickness. As if my gall bladder had released its bitter juices into my system from where they infiltrated my heart. That was only the beginning. Waves of revulsion, a terrible urge to empty my stomach and bowels then and there. Not in front of the men and the Process Inspector. Certainly not in front of the Easties! That shame would destroy me. I steadied myself by locking my gaze onto the eyes of the farmer portrayed in the large painting on the wall opposite. In her arms was a lamb, loved and protected. The farmer's eyes reached out and held me fast. 'What have you done?' they asked. 'What have you done?'

I distinctly remember leaving my body and rising up to one of the entrance hall chandeliers. From that lofty position I looked down and saw the men, the Process Inspector, the suitcases and bags, the offspring, the shattered mother, the body, the blood, and then, where I should have been, was a <u>something</u>. That version of myself might have passed as human had it not lacked a few vital elements. A being without empathy, stripped of love and understanding, is an ugly creature. We try hard never to see this side of ourselves.

Eventually the mother's screams evolved into a howl. Spine-tingling notes of pain and disbelief escaped from deep within her chest. The sound rattled the windows and worried my nerves. In the meantime, my airborne self, because it had nowhere else to go, returned to the ground. All present watched as I returned the pistol to its holster, and then lit up a cigarette. My hands were as steady and calm as a mountain. On the inside, the banalities of emotion ground my soul into dust. 'What are you?' 'I am a God!'

I felt sorry for the now youngest male. Events had caused him to spontaneously soil his garments. I suggested a change of clothing, and sent him off with two of the men to clean up and find something appropriate to wear. He moved in a sequence of slow-motion jerks, a fragile, rickety puppet.

A quarter of an hour later, I granted the family permission to take the carcass with them to their next destination. The men had since removed the remains from the property, dragged it across the front garden, out through the gate, and deposited it on the pavement. A few neighbours came to the family's aid. Terrified Easties scurried one way and the other, doing all in their power to avoid my gaze. Using a combination of curtains, bedsheets and native skills, the carcass was packaged up and hoisted onto one of the Unlawful Resident Transfer Squad's trucks.

I stood erect and proud, under the trees outside No. 17. I puffed on my cigarette and observed the comings and goings. The bits and pieces of the world around me appeared far away. Back then I felt powerful, today I feel unclean. What manner of being takes pride in acting this way?

The rest of the day's Site Inspections were, thankfully, uneventful. We got on with the business of dispensing official Declarations of Illegality, the recipients got on with the business of vacating Ministry of Housing and Justice property. My feet carried me from one inspection site to the next. My lips moved, my tongue wagged, orders left my mouth. I was simultaneously present and absent. The outside world saw an officer of the NDM, functioning in a truly professional manner. On the inside, I felt nauseous.

That night, I, who never went beyond slightly tipsy, returned home late and very drunk. I could barely stand. The next morning over breakfast, with my head still ringing like church bells, you shared the story of me staggering in, practically foaming at the mouth, and raging incessantly about a pan of stew. My obsession with the pan was such, you wondered if my work had given me a mental attack. 'What do you mean?' I challenged you. Your response was to recite a list of the ways in which I had changed. I recognized nothing. You talked of a night in ruins. Dinner cold, efforts wasted. I apologized for letting dinner slip my mind. 'Has the NDM banned anniversaries?' you asked. I dared not reveal the circumstances that led me to forget. Instead, I produced a vague fable about the Eastie rabble-rousers we caught harassing some of our women and children. That was a lie. Every word nonsense. But you knew, your laugh said it all.

From the moment we left No. 17, not only was I plagued with a growing sense that I had shrunk in the world, but also by the constant echo of the mother's howls. Her sorrow filled my head and would not leave. Equally disturbing, I heard a voice within my head, and one I could not recognize, ask over and over again: 'What have you done? What have you done?'

I replaced my blood with liquor, then grabbed that whiny voice by the throat and strangled it. You mentioned how that night I howled out like some wild creature. I claimed to have no knowledge of this. In truth, I was wide awake. The cry marked the moment I let go of most that was good in me. And then, miracle of miracles, I slept like a man with no worries, without a conscience as ballast. I now understand that not all doors remain open when you pass through: some close behind you forever.

I made my choices. There was no coercion, no

enforcement. The sad conclusion was that I, with my supposed broad world-view and education, was not immune to the effects of nationalist euphoria sweeping across our land. With practically everyone else doing the same, I learned to act without thinking, and remained happily blind to the greater consequences of my choices. Back then it was easy to believe my actions, no matter how abhorrent, had the blessing of the nation, the NDM and Our Dear Leader. I delegated my thinking to Our Dear Leader, the top echelons of the NDM and to DIDS. It was easy to do so.

The delivery of official Declarations of Illegality and extraction of illegal Eastie occupants, driven by our use of 'all available resources', became a blood sport. I played without resistance or hesitation. We were officers of the NDM and guardians of the land. The occasional dead Eastie was an acceptable price to pay for national security and survival.

Today, and far too late to be of much use to you, I understand how thoroughly miserable the two months following the incident at No. 17 must have been for you. I lost count of how many times you pleaded with me to explain what was wrong. How often did you, in tears, declare my behaviour to be cold and without love or mercy? I remember that terrible argument, when you challenged me to find some other work, something that would not consume every gram of joy. I listened, but could not hear. One by one, the strands binding us together frayed. Your visits became less frequent. Our conversations became hot with the friction of differences. 'How can you not see them as fellow human beings?' More command than question. 'How can you blame everyone for the behaviour of a few?' Your increasingly sympathetic views of the Easties clashed with my understanding of the species. You spouted radical dogma. You claimed a culture or language could be different to, but never greater than, another. I countered with a memorized list of established truths. Back and forth we argued. Ever louder until the moment, at our wits' end, we agreed to disagree, and lapsed into an uncomfortable silence. Volatile was a fair description of our relationship. And then Our Dear Leader issued the Final Ultimatum. It was a welcome move.

The tense and soured relationship between ourselves and the East worsened. Barbed, ugly and passive-aggressive insults were tossed back and forth, like sticky mud, between our capitals. The Easties called us robbers, snakes and oppressors of their people. We, in turn, referred to them as corrupt, barbaric fools. Such was the state of our coexistence until one day, Our Dear Leader, backed by the NDM, decided enough was enough. He looked East and spoke: 'Neighbours to our East, our patience has come to an end, and justice is on the way. It can visit the few, or affect the many. The choice is yours.' On behalf of the NDM and the nation, Our Dear Leader issued a Final Ultimatum to the Eastern leadership. They were given seventy-two hours to hand over those responsible for the Dear Leader's assassination. Failure to comply within the allotted time frame automatically gave us the right to act in a manner that protected our honour and national interests.

The distraction of the Final Ultimatum provided an escape route from the constant examination of our personal relationship. There was an ominous ring to Our Dear Leader's voice. One newspaper columnist described it as 'the song of tempered steel leaving its sheath'. The nation listened and prepared. The state of affairs between us and the East demanded most of my attention. You stepped back, gave me room. A gap appeared between us.

14

War was coming. We could feel it, we smelled it. As hot metal: angry and dangerous. War called out from radio speakers across the land, channelled through Our Dear Leader's speeches. Each transmission was twice as fiery as the one before. War attached itself to every other newspaper headline. War infiltrated the games of children playing in their neighbourhood streets and the city's parks. War attached itself to the lyrics of popular songs. War influenced the fashions of the day: even household items were not immune. War adjusted our way of thinking and looking at the world. War rumbled in the accelerating mobilization. It beckoned the nation's young men (I among them), and promised adventure filled with glory of historical proportions. Still smarting from having missed out on the action in the previous conflict, of course I leapt at the opportunity.

Military vehicles became a regular part of city traffic. Our national ensign fluttered from flagpoles that seemed to sprout out of every facade and half the city's rooftops.

NDM forces, in their thousands and thousands, marched towards our eastern border. The nation looked on at the tanks, the guns, the men in their uniforms, and wept with pride. We were so much more than a war machine. We were a statement of intent. We were magnificent. We were power! The nation sent us off with cheers and wishes for a speedy victory. I saw the flags and listened to the joyous bands. Everyone loved us, with the exception of the Easties among us. They too watched, powerless and afraid, as we headed off to destroy their land.

Behind the noise and exuberance, behind my upright, eyes-forward pose, was a sorrow. An aching heart. We had been apart for two and a half, three weeks. Seeing you again gave me such warmth. Were it not for my uniform, and the need to maintain standards, I might have cried. I had missed you, though not as painfully as I do now. I remember my sisters, who thought I did not know they had arranged for you to come to say goodbye, fidgeting and giggling in the background. I remember your fingers touching my uniform, here, here, there . . . I remember your eyes. They revealed your sadness at my leaving (we had yet to smooth out matters between us) and worry about the nature of my adventure. Finally came your parting gift: this journal, and a request that I make a record of my travels.

I headed east with the Property and Population Control Battalion, also known as the PPC. Our battalion flag was dark maroon with a large golden circle in the middle. The circle, which also served as our shoulder sleeve insignia, contained a graphic representation of a house with a family inside. As was expected of anything developed by NDM Messaging and Public Relations, the design had a certain visual clarity: almost friendly. We were also provided with 'complimentary' cards, one side of which carried our battalion flag while the other bore the simple text: 'Approved by NDM Property and Population Control'.

I fear the PPC's contribution to the history books will be written in red ink. Something happened as we crossed the Eastern border. We threw off the part of ourselves that recognized the 'other' as human, jettisoned our conscience as if it were excess baggage.

By the time our armies were unleashed on the East, the language used to describe Easties had become vicious and extremely ugly. Stories about Easties in our nation being spat upon, beaten and worse, had become too common to make the news. As we soldiers of the NDM moved into the East, every one of us did so in the understanding we had entered a land inhabited by savages, an inferior category of human being. This being the case, our moral codes did not apply in the East.

Our Dear Leader compelled us to go forward, to become legends, to write our glorious chapter in the history books! He commanded us to scorch the earth beneath our enemy's feet, and then drench the ashes with Eastie blood. As hungry demons, we swallowed these words and nourished ourselves with what they implied.

The Easties' large, lumbering forces were no match for our agility and brutality, or for our discipline and focus. The superior firepower of the NDM troops, combined with tactics developed during and after our war with the West, allowed us to roll over their legions with ease. In addition, all NDM soldiers believed we fought for a superior purpose: the Greater Glory. The heady essence of one victory after another turned our minds and rendered our every action correct. I am sure you know what it is to win and succeed, in school, at work, in life . . . You remember the accompanying glow, warm and magnificent. The sense of floating above all others. I assure you, the thrill of defeating an army and reducing it to a memory is a thousand times greater than any of that.

Our behaviour in this land, and the PPC's existence, can be understood in the context of Our Dear Leader's belief that the removal of everything worth fighting for would break the spirit, and a broken people would have no will to resist. Prior to his ascension, Our Dear Leader had run the Ministry of Data and Security's Office of Strategic Possibilities. We referred to them as the 'What Ifs'. They used analysis from EDS and DIDS data streams as input for the generation of a seemingly unlimited range of possible scenarios: What if this? What if that? It was as Head of Strategic Possibilities that Our Dear Leader had developed the scenario of 'Erasure'.

He viewed 'identity' as a complex cement that held a people together. Identity included language, traditions, music, art, industry, and so on. Any single one, or a combination of these elements could be employed as 'fuel' to encourage resistance to external forces. An example of this was the use of our own warrior ancestry to rally the nation, and ultimately defeat the Westerners, during the last war.

The complete erasure of such elements, in a wartime setting, would allow for swifter victories. Furthermore, over time erasure could 'disappear' a people from history.

At the time, our since-deceased head of state, the Dear Leader, declared it a scenario conjured up by the Devil, and reminded those concerned that the Office of Strategic Possibilities was <u>not</u> the place for such thinking. The NDM's purpose was to facilitate growth and improvement. In short: to build, and not destroy. Now the brain behind the Erasure Doctrine belonged to our new man at the top. He was the law and believed, in the context of their deeds, and supported by the demands of justice, that erasure was an appropriate fate for the Easties.

The PPC became my home, and still remains so, though our current numbers would barely fill a platoon. We are the militarized arm of the Property Integrity Office. We report to the Ministry of Data and Security, rather than the Ministry of Defence, and are one of the NDM's 'special units'. The special units were a natural evolution of the action teams set up within Data and Security to carry out <u>hands-on</u>, rather than <u>administrative</u> tasks. When the need arose, the PPC performed duties in conjunction with regular NDM Army or Flying Forces.

Most of the time, as was the case with all other special units, we operated alone.

Some of the great tales of our time contain references to structures and cities that have long since disappeared. One hoped for by-product of our conquering the East would be the total erasure of their culture. The task given to the PPC was to focus on objects and structures of interest. These included architectural highlights, industry, art, museum artefacts, etc. We methodically recorded every last detail of what we believed worthy during our Property and Population Inspections, and then destroyed them. Our documentation was sent, via messenger, back to the Ministry of Data and Security. The photographs and filmed footage were analysed, categorized, and then given a quiet home in the vast Data and Security archives. There were also reports. Some made their way back to the PPC in the form of advised adjustments to specific methods: increased efficiency the goal, as always.

The PPC earned the nickname 'The Factory Boys' because of the huge mobile processing units that accompanied us. Our stone grinders transformed even the most stubborn materials into gravel. Our furnaces dealt with all leftover metals. We could smelt anything, from structural iron down to the precious solids found in museum pieces. For more menial duties, such as glass collection, book, fabric and wood burning, we employed able-bodied members of the local population.

Strictly speaking, the PPC is not a fighting battalion. Though when challenged or harassed in any way, we strike back. In the early days of the invasion, we fought alongside the 13th Armoured Battalion. However, within a week, the PPC was busy going about what we were created to do: recording and then destroying any item an Eastie might be proud of. Erasure.

The PPC became notorious for its scorched rubble blessings. There is a hypnotic quality to demolition, and a spirituality to the dismantling of splendour. We carried out orders, distilled from the words of Our Dear Leader, with great fervour. By the time we had completed our eighth or ninth inspection, turning objects into ashes and/or rubble had become a near-religious experience for the soldiers of the PPC. Meanwhile, the wanton destruction fed the wild within us. The beauty of much that we smashed was breathtaking. We created ruin, and then laughed at the Easties as they watched what we did and wept. The rout of the Eastern armies gave us the room to operate as we pleased. We believed our actions were those of higher beings, dishing out civilization to inferior creatures. Clearing out the waste in preparation for a more enlightened infrastructure. I am no longer able to see our behaviour as anything other than violent thuggery, perpetrated by men in finely tailored uniforms.

The East surprised me in many ways, the most notable of which was the architecture. Here were structures and proportions I had never seen before. The Easties appeared to have invented new colours and materials for their buildings. It was fascinating. Primitive, of course, and yet something about their constructions always caught my eye. Such a shame you and I never managed to travel in the East, back when our countries were still at peace. Perhaps there is some twisted consolation in being one of the last people alive to see these buildings, paintings, sculptures, and so on, in their full glory.

I ordered destruction with the excitement of a child who has just learned the joy of knocking down building blocks. I remember once, on holiday, Mother scolding a child on the beach. The boy, a little older than I, had come along and smashed the sandcastle complex my friends and

I had spent the afternoon constructing. 'How can you be happy breaking up what others have made?' she asked. I cannot remember the boy's answer. What would Mother have to say about my work here in the East? We soldiers of the PPC certainly knew how to demolish with glee. Our battalion was home to some of our nation's finest engineering minds. With bittersweet pride, I tell you these men came up with the most ingenious methods of reducing buildings to dust. No structure could withstand their destructive creativity.

The NDM High Command believed we were doing an exemplary job and complimented us on our inspirational and outstanding work. Their words gave us a boost, confirmed our belief in the righteousness of our mission for the Greater Glory, and in our sense of invincibility. This state of mind prepared us for the next phase of our mission. We were truly unstoppable.

One problem that confronts armies in the case of rapid territorial gain is what to do with the civilians, the stragglers and others caught up in our bloody business. NDM High Command understood military efficiency was achieved through a combination of factors, one being the careful management of resources. The wretched hordes of Eastie prisoners were a problem. Initially, we fed and sheltered the captives in rudimentary compounds, as per the conventions of war. Meanwhile, NDM High Command, in consultation with Our Dear Leader, made the necessary decisions. Ever-increasing food consumption by an ever-multiplying number of prisoners was seen as an unnecessary drain. The Easties were hungry: they ate as if food would be declared illegal within the hour. There were even a number of jokes in circulation themed around the Eastie plan to defeat us by consuming all our provisions! NDM High Command provided a simple and effective solution: they declared the continued management of Eastie holding compounds a needless waste of valuable resources. Commanding officers of the special units were given freedom to resolve matters relating to overconsumption as they saw fit. Our rules of engagement were adjusted to reflect this new flexibility. Additionally, improved manufacturing technology back home, and an efficient logistics network, kept us well supplied with bullets. At the time I understood the logic behind these choices. However, I was less understanding of our battalion's diversion away from straightforward erasure to 'prisoner management' duties.

To call the endless killing of captives <u>boring</u> may sound callous, even mad to your ears.

Unfortunately, bored is how we felt, and killing is what we did.

Such work is never easy, in the beginning. But in time, because we are soldiers loyal to the NDM, we learned to remove our actions from the clutches of conscience and emotion. All for the Greater Glory.

I heard a rumour, we all did, that Our Dear Leader paid a visit to one such prisoner management enclosure to get a first-hand glimpse of Eastie erasure in action. They say he watched and immediately took ill when the first body hit the floor of the burial trench. They whisked him away and sent him home in a flash, so the rumour goes. Word came down from NDM HQ warning us to ignore any 'cowardly gossip' about Our Dear Leader as this was the creation of 'filthy Eastie tongues'. We listened, we shrugged our collective shoulders, and then got on with our work.

Were our activities ever to appear in a work of fiction, any readers with stomachs hardy enough to read through to the end might call it a vivid depiction of Lucifer's work. The reality is otherwise. The Devil had nothing to do with our business. Every one of us functioned as expected, as elite soldiers with a clear objective. We slaughtered and shed blood with a delirious pride. We developed new methods of killing. Our murderous experimentation, more often than not, had <u>little</u> to do with tactics or efficiency and <u>a lot</u> to do with keeping the men entertained.

I was present at all times. I questioned nothing, resisted nothing. I saw to it our orders were carried out to the letter, and often led by example. Whenever doubt or a hint of conscience threatened to raise its head, I chased it off with a reminder that 'I am a God' and that all our actions were for the Greater Glory. Our souls, meanwhile, began to rot. The stench of spiritual decay was always about us. On our skin, on our uniforms, in the air, and in the results of our endeavours. How glad we were when the battalion returned to our regular erasure business.

For long stretches of our journey, there was no enemy to fight, and nothing to destroy. The bored men often shot at passing birds, or anything else that lived and moved. Others succumbed to a melancholy and claimed to no longer understand what they were doing, or why we were there. A gentle chat, and a reminder to honour their uniforms and focus on the Greater Glory, was usually enough to snap them out of their gloom. Though I did see their point: we were trained for action. Unfortunately, our destruction of the Eastern army saw us capture territory without resistance. There was little glory in that.

As exciting as destruction can be, smashing and breaking and crushing, day after day, does become monotonous. I noticed an increase in the number of errors and delays during operations. The reasons for the slips were often related to lapses in focus. This I reported back up the chain of command. I was met with understanding. The men of the PPC were not alone in suffering the tedium brought on by the Easties' military weakness and cowardice. This condition afflicted most of the NDM forces in the East. Boredom aside, in the bigger scheme of the war, I had noticed (in the same manner we note the approach of spring) the appearance of the first shoots of total victory. Glory approached. I could feel it in my bones, and heard it in the tone of messages between ourselves and High Command. I shared this insight with the men: 'Have patience. It is just a matter of time.' These were good men. They heard me. We marched further east, crushing and ripping apart every object of beauty that lay in our path.

The sheer size of the country was awe-inspiring and,

at times, menacing. The distance between towns and cities of interest appeared infinite. Imagine travelling for days through a landscape that does not change. At first, the endless sameness is hypnotic, almost soothing. But it soon becomes maddening. Everything we saw appeared to constantly transform into what we had just seen! The unchanging scenery made us question whether we were moving at all. I will never forget the unvarying crunch and groan of tracks and wheels, the rumble of engines and thud of booted feet as we moved through kilometre after kilometre of sun-bleached land. Thankfully, there were occasions when the monotony of the landscape was temporarily interrupted by an unusual geographic feature.

One moment. Aircraft approaching! I need to go out. I shall return soon.

15

What can I tell you? I have spent the last three minutes or so waiting for my fingers to stop trembling. The aircraft have gone. Rather than soften us up with bombs, or pepper our positions with bullets, they showered us with sheets of paper. Questionnaires! The enemy plays with us. At the top of each sheet was a crude illustration: a caricature of Our Dear Leader engaged in an act too foul for these pages, his partner in this activity being a dog. Beneath the image was text written in our language. 'Dear Animals of the NDM, please choose your manner of death. Encircle one of the options below and present it to our troops as they arrive.' Below, a list of options, A to D, described various ways to butcher a human being. Each more vicious than the one before. All very slow. I had nothing to say to the men. I could not lie and pretend these were idle threats.

One of our sergeants offered a witty comment regarding our enemy's originality. As a result, some of the recently recruited boy-soldiers began to weep. I understood. We longer-serving men had willingly signed up for this adventure, these unfortunate children had not. Press-ganged by the NDM into military service, thrown into this misery. And to what end? Their short lives will never see victory. They cannot fight. They slow us down. We are soldiers, not mothers! Goodness knows what madness reigns in NDM High Command. How can they not understand, sending children into battle is mass murder? Do they not have children of their own, or younger brothers? I am thankful my sisters were not the brothers I always wished for. How would I have protected them from this horror? One boy-soldier was in such a state, I had to comfort him as I would a child lost in the city. Frail and terrified, his every muscle trembled, including the ones controlling his lips. He asked me to save him. What could I do, send a bullet through his skull once the enemy began its final assault? I kissed his forehead, and then whispered hollow encouragements in his ear.

On the way back to the tent, I considered how the boy was beyond my help, and realized the same applied to myself. I no longer have influence over anything except the attitude with which I accept the end. Death is coming soon. The questionnaires from the sky confirmed this. I sat down, tried to write, and fear attacked my fingers. The others in the tent were too wrapped up in their own business to notice.

It occurs to me that among the reverential tales of our ancestral warriors who gave their lives for this, that and the other, not one tells us what these heroes felt or thought just before death carried them off.

I was about to describe to you one incident that made quite an impression on us, as we trundled through the unchanging landscape. Believe it or not, here and there in this abattoir, there are a few gentler moments. The morning after we first began to worry about the effects of geographic monotony on the men's spirits, Fate blessed us with a change of scenery. Our joy was infectious and exuberant. Imagine a whole battalion of men jumping about and whooping as if they had stumbled across the pot of gold at the rainbow's end.

The first indication was the change in colour of the long grasses, from bleached gold-brown to a green so lush, it took a fair amount of self-control to keep from ordering the driver to stop. I wished to step out and run through the grass! The expressions on the faces of the men around me made it clear I was not alone in harbouring such thoughts. Many of the infantrymen were unable to control themselves. Like children, they ran through the grass and released their inner foolishness. The ground beneath our feet marked the beginning of a long, slow descent into a valley, the likes of which we had never seen.

In the stories about ancient times, they talk of mighty beings with fists the size of mountains. The valley around us could well be the work of one such giant. Imagine the giant, in a fit of boredom, scraping a finger along the Earth's crust, much as we once did with our own fingers through damp sand at the water's edge. True, our country is home to many areas of natural beauty: the Southern Forest, the Highland Caves, not to mention the countless botanical gardens throughout the land. Trust me, all of that is mud compared to the beauty of this valley.

The flowers and shrubs were of completely alien shades, shapes and sizes. The sight of this flora filled our eyes with tears and our hearts with a sense of triumph. Another item of note was the absence of any paths or tracks in the valley. We felt like pioneers conquering lands usually left well alone by humankind. The sight of our battalion snaking its way through the valley was impressive indeed. I knew the image of our efficient, deadly serpent of war against the surrounding glory would impress those back home. I asked the photographers and camera crew trucks to circle around and record the PPC crossing the valley.

The noise of an army on the move is an assault on the ears. Engines, motors, caterpillar tracks, all manner of wheels, shouted commands, radio chatter, laughter, crunching boots, mechanical clatter, all combine into a symphony of dread. Enough to set the most committed pacifist's heart aflutter. This was not the case in the valley. The clangour of our battle-thirsty machine was drowned out by Nature's song. Our noise fell away as the sound of the wind and birds and crickets filled the audible foreground. I assumed this was an illusory effect created by the gently swaying grasses and the height of the valley's walls.

We travelled for a day and a half through the valley. I had never imagined it possible to descend to such depths yet remain above ground. The increased distance between ourselves and the sky above gave it an extraordinary blue tint. The sun, while bright and intense as ever, did not scorch us. As we crossed the valley's lowest point, a twenty-odd-kilometre stretch, the size of the walls to our north and south made us shrink. I believed, though I did not share this idea with anyone else, Mother Nature was giving a gentle reminder: on this globe, we humans, with our toys and manners, are not that important. A humbling experience, if ever there was one.

The final ten kilometres of the valley were even more impressive. The ground began to rise, and as it did so, trees appeared. A few here, some there, and there . . . Soon we found ourselves moving through a seemingly endless forest. The trees were magnificent, great in size and varied in attitude: proud trees, angry trees, laughing trees, dancing trees, quiet trees, wise trees. The trees must have been there at humanity's birth, and would still be around long after our demise. Had circumstances been otherwise, we would have stopped and taken the time to examine the forest. The experience of standing close to one of those mighty trees would have been quite a thrill.

16

With great sadness and shame, I can safely conclude that no other creature on this globe has butchered and drenched the soil in blood as we have. Yes, every action we took was for the good of the nation, but there is a price to pay for this. In the belief we had no choice but to distance ourselves from all emotional distractions, we became men of rock and iron, charged with carrying out actions and performing duties that lay beyond the abilities of ordinary citizens.

'What are you?' 'I am a God!'

We were reacquainted with the more stubborn Easties midway through their country. Our contact began with the occasional pocket of brief resistance. A skirmish here, another there. Always quickly snuffed out. Always a few casualties on our side: unfortunate and unnecessary. We were told their stubborn behaviour was a telltale sign of a simple, frightened mind. One unable to grasp, and therefore <u>see</u>, the reality before it. The reality was our cultural, intellectual and, of course, military superiority. Swollen with victory's arrogance, we failed to see the method in the Easties' mosquito warfare. A bite here, another there. A minor loss. Another minor loss. At the time we believed the Easties were very good at hiding the bodies of their dead. We rarely discovered any. Did we fight with invisible men? We found the Eastie style irritating, of course, but ultimately considered it ineffective. Our progress was irresistible. We could never be stopped. So we believed.

Today, I can do nothing but laugh at our annoyance and complaints regarding Eastie tactics. We called them unscrupulous vandals. We believed no action was too low or underhand for an Eastie. Whatever they called that 'business' of theirs, it was <u>not</u> warfare. It was scandalous. Baited traps in buildings, in animals. Bodies of our fallen rigged with explosive. If ever proof was needed that Easties belonged at the more primitive end of humanity's scale, it was plain to see in their despicable conduct. As the Easties' devious attacks on NDM forces increased, so did our loathing of them as living creatures. This evolution in our thinking was reflected in the escalating vindictiveness of our reprisals. Our Dear Leader and the top rungs of the NDM believed revenge, when employed with planning and precision, was an effective means of communication. In the case of the Easties, the special units, such as the PPC, used revenge to make it clear there was no equality between us. We meted out vengeance as if only we had the right to do so. If, for example, they killed one of us, we replied by executing ten of their number, selected at random.

Now, I realize that revenge is heavy work. My eyes and ears have seen too much. The misery, the terror, the blood. The cries of mothers with screaming children, weeping sisters, terrified brothers, fathers, aunts, uncles, friends . . . Desperation. Everyone wants to survive. I watched Easties beg and humiliate themselves as if shame did not exist. Anything for an extra second of life.

The threat of death gives birth to the strangest actions. The Easties always found one or two of their number who spoke our language well enough to be understood. Some believed this ability gave them the right to extra privileges, such as not joining the others in burial trenches. Hopeful translators offered us jewellery, money, property . . . We always laughed at that. As if soldiers of the PPC had time for, or interest in such items. They offered their assistance on matters of communication. We declined. Our orders were clear. We allowed Easties to keep hold of their worldly goods as we sent them off to that other place.

As I write of who I was then (a champion of our bloody business, aiming my weapon and pulling the trigger), there are moments when I am forced to pause. I touch these pages, my chest, my face. I look about me. The tent, the men and our circumstances confirm the truth. My actions brought us here, and as for how I managed to carry out such deeds with ease and pleasure, I do not know. Perhaps my mind at the time was preoccupied with thoughts of process and efficiency. Today it is visited by a troubling observation: all Easties looked and sounded very human to me.

17

An afternoon during what became my final trip home springs to mind. It is already thirteen months in the past! I wandered around the city without a plan. We had parted that morning with more anger than love. The cause of our friction was the foreign media and their lies about our war with the East. You challenged me, as you had throughout my visit, about these news articles. How much of what they said was true? I gave you a lecture on politics and devious propaganda. You called me blind and a puppet: a cheap clone of Our Dear Leader. I had no time for such nonsense and stormed out.

While out walking, I found myself surprised by the number of never before seen buildings, pavements, lampposts, neighbourhood parks, etc. I, with my supposed eye for detail, born and raised in this town, saw everything in a brand-new, quite beautiful light. Stranger still, I remember my eyes drinking it in, as if they were afraid to forget. From this position, it is as if Fate already knew . . .

My wanderings were interrupted by two schoolboys,

aged around nine or ten. They accosted me, announced their plans to become future heroes of the NDM, and asked for tips on how to make this happen. I became stuck. Whatever I had become at this point, I was not so far gone as to encourage the boys to take the same path as myself. At the same time, I had no desire to throw cold water on their dreams. The indecision that had plagued me prior to joining the NDM made a brief return. The result: paralysis. I stared at the boys. They stared back.

Eventually, and thankfully, the boys quickly removed us from the slightly awkward situation. They asked, in unison (as if the question had been posed many times before): 'How did <u>you</u> become a hero?' The question caught me flat-footed. These children still believed war was all guns and glory. I chose not to share the truth, and claimed to have pressing business elsewhere. I wished the two boys a pleasant afternoon and went on my way. Were they to see me now!

It was not long after this final trip home that Fate intervened to set up a meeting between the PPC and the 2nd Armoured Division. Our operations were such that we required a certain distance and disconnection from regular

NDM forces. All were happy with this arrangement, so this coincidence was an unusual affair. It took place early afternoon, eleven months ago. Our battalion was headed in a south-by-east direction, en route to a Property and Population Inspection: a small town, population approximately eight and a half thousand, though of great spiritual importance to the Easties. National folklore had this town as the birthplace of all things Eastie. Every one of them, at some point in their lives, visited the town to pay their respects. Our mission, following the usual recordings for later analysis, was complete erasure.

In the relentless push for efficiency, the strategists upstairs believed employing the NDM Flying Forces during the initial erasure phase would save time and materiel. Needless to say, our engineers and demolition teams were none too pleased. 'How accurate are the bombers?' they asked. 'What about unexploded ordnance?' We sent these and many other questions to NDM High Command. In reply, we were reminded of Our Dear Leader's expectation that officers of the NDM set an example to others and follow orders to the letter, without exception. We relayed this to the men, though in a milder tone. They accepted with grumbles. One of the engineers likened the use of aerial bombardment to an attempt at rendering an oil landscape with a tree trunk instead of a natural hair brush. We all got a laugh out of that.

The situation was as follows: the 1st, 4th and 5th Companies of the PPC were two hours ahead. We had remained behind with 3rd Company while they dealt with broken tracks on a number of their tanks. Problems solved, we moved on.

The region was free from enemy forces, and due to our preference for invisibility, Comms had cleared all regular military traffic from the area. We expected unhindered and unobserved passage. Unfortunately, Comms had not taken into account our two-hour delay. We approached the second to last crossroads before our final destination and found it blocked by the 2nd Armoured Division, travelling in an adjacent direction. Our initial response, as we were in no great hurry, was to wait. Motors were turned off as the caravan of troops and tanks and whatnot passed by.

As we waited, not a single hand was raised in salute, and not once did we receive a nod of acknowledgement. This in spite of our own salutes. The soldiers of the 2nd Armoured either ignored us, or looked upon us with disgust. As if we in the PPC were in some way inferior to them. We knew the rumours about regular NDM forces' disapproval of our methods. There were some who believed our actions had nothing to do with war. To such men, I would give a simple reminder: war evolves together with its participants. Today's armies behave and fight in a very different manner to those of a thousand years past. Other members of the regular forces argued our methods would bring shame and darkness upon the nation. The weakness in character displayed by those harbouring such thoughts was evident in the fact not one of them ever came and presented such an argument to my face.

The disregard of our salutes and our presence made us feel quite foolish. This treatment meted out by the 2nd Armoured was a thorny insult, as they punctured and then deflated our pride. We knew the role played by the special units in this war for the Greater Glory was just as important, if not more so, than that of anyone else. Yet, as a reward, we received silence and scowls from our very own brothers in arms! Rejection by one's own is an uncomfortable experience.

I now understand that the source of our discomfort was the sight of what we had become reflected back at us in the expressions of the 2nd Armoured soldiers. Not one of us had the desire to ask why the disdain was there. No need. We knew. The PPC battalion killed the old and unarmed, the weak, the scared. Men, women, children, infants. Meanwhile, many, like the two curious lads on my last trip home, looked upon men like myself and saw glory! With its array of colour-coded ribbons, those boys saw in my uniform an action hero from their comic books. They did not see the rot inside. How could they?

I cannot tell you what brings greater sadness: the results of my deeds, or the fact I performed every act without the slightest hint of shame or glimmer of mercy. Charity, compassion and sanctity of life were not words found in the PPC lexicon. That afternoon, the meeting with 2nd Armoured put us all in a very dark mood.

En route to the crossroads, about thirty minutes to the rear, we had spotted an odd-looking hill to our west. It was covered with a patchwork of crop and grazing fields, connected by a series of paths leading up to the small village at its summit. That a village should exist out in this emptiness, far from any other population centres, stirred my interest. The distance between our position and the village made it impossible to pick out much of the detail.

Though we did notice how no two buildings shared the same colour. Given that our business was elsewhere, we decided the village was too remote, too small, too insignificant. Dropping by for a visit was out of the question.

After fifteen minutes of chewing dust, I realized the 2nd Armoured, travelling along a road such as this, would take hours to pass. There was also a growing restlessness among the men, as the sting of wounded pride made itself known. Not all questions have simple answers. I cannot tell you why I allowed my insulted ego to play a role in the choices I made. Neither can I say why it was necessary to whip up such blood-red enthusiasm for an impromptu Property and Population Inspection. But I did, and I <u>did</u>. We decided to about-turn, head north, and pay the funny little village a visit after all.

18

The village occupants spotted us long before we arrived. There was nothing unusual about this. It was, after all, their terrain. As we approached the hill's summit (we were on foot, having parked our equipment in a large circle around the hill's base), a curious herd of goats came to inspect us, and then, with much bleating and tinkling of bells, escorted us into the village. Surprisingly, our arrival was greeted with cheers and applause! I would say close to three hundred and fifty occupants lined the main path into the village.

The village occupants showered us with dry grass and fuchsia-coloured petals. I still remember the dusty, salty fragrance of the grass. As for the petals . . . I plucked a few from my sleeve and rubbed them between my fingertips. They left behind a lightly tinted and oily residue. I sniffed at my fingers, and a blast of sweet-perfumed gasoline made me dizzy. Powerful stuff! The scent of dry grass and the petals combined to produce a heady welcome.

Easties welcoming the PPC into their village as if we

were heroes was simply unheard of. Had the world turned itself upside down? Believe it or not, one of the village occupants held aloft a framed photograph of none other than Our Dear Leader! The photograph captured him midway through what appeared to be a rant. Such <u>expressive</u> portraits of Our Dear Leader never appeared in the media back home. For a few seconds I believed the war had torn my mind to shreds and created a whole new reality. One in which the local population recieved death with joy and open arms. However, as I stood and conversed with a committee of five elders, I noticed all was not quite what it seemed. There was a familiar tension in their eye and body movements.

Given our activities in the East, the PPC's reputation brought terror to even the bravest souls. Hidden behind our clinically bureaucratic appellation ('Property and Population Control' did have a certain officious neutrality to it) was the destructive rage of wild, conscienceless animals. NDM High Command strategists believed in the importance of the psychological impact of our actions, an effect amplified by the near absence of survivors. By this stage in the war, the end phase of our Property and Population Inspections involved targeting anything that lived or moved. The aim, beyond erasing everything of value, was to fill the hearts of the Easties with absolute dread.

When the PPC arrived at a village or town and rounded up those who had not managed to run away, the atmosphere was usually one of anguish and desperation. Unfortunate natives filled the air with sounds of suppressed panic. I believe their restraint in expressing honest emotion had much to do with the myth that refusal to show fear could keep one alive. Perhaps there had been a few circumstances in which this was the case, though never in any situation involving the PPC. On occasion, usually driven by wickedness or boredom, we did nothing but wait and see how long before those left behind lost their composure. The impending collapse in decorum would be announced by a few random whimpers, and then moans, followed by squeals, cries, pleading. There was always plenty of weeping, begging and self-humiliation. At times the situation got so out of hand, we ended up with hordes of blabbering Easties prostrating themselves on the ground before us. That was not the case on this particular afternoon.

*

Once the village occupants' cheering and noise had calmed down (the anxious background chatter never stopped), I engaged in further conversation with the village elders. The exchange was facilitated by one of their females, whose age I would place between twenty and twenty-five years. She surprised us with her fluency in our tongue. As she spoke, her words sang to us, and we remembered home. How the female learned our language will forever remain a mystery.

We usually had little to say to the natives, but on occasion, when the mood took us, we chatted for a while before commencing our business. These 'conversations' were primarily for aesthetic purposes. Our photographers clicked away and recorded the always helpful, always friendly PPC soldiers chatting merrily with the natives. The themes of our talks were usually light-hearted matters: weather, the cost of living, family . . . That afternoon, the bulk of our conversation was filled with an endless stream of compliments from the village elders. These were expressed through a series of hisses and sounds from the back of the throat. Theirs was a strange dialect, quite unlike the usual Eastie noises. It conjured up visions in my head of ancient and primitive times. We learned how happy the occupants were to see us. How proud they were that we chose to bless them with our presence. They believed we were great warriors and virtuous men, and in honour of this, the village had prepared a toast.

You remember my allergy to loud public compliments? This is Mother's doing. Never one for acclamation, her approval was expressed with a hug, a kiss, a touch, a glance. The louder the praise, she claimed, the less it had to do with the receiver, and the more it involved the giver's need for attention. I looked at the village elders and noted their strained jollity. They did not seek attention, they sought a way to remain alive.

I watched the elders: their eagerness to please us returned me to a moment in high school. One slow-moving afternoon, during the last term of the school year, I sat passing time with some of the school's rougher characters. Back then, as was my way, I had complete freedom of movement between the school's various tribes. The sun was hot and bright, and we sat in the shade under the trees at the north end of the school fields, where the grass was soft, fresh and summer green. I was tuned into an animated conversation about motorcycles, when a junior student appeared and put an end to the chatter. It must have been an unforgettable moment for the unfortunate pupil. In his right hand was a large bag of goodies. He clenched it tight. On his left side, gripped firmly between upper arm and chest, were three bottles of fizzy drinks. Given our senior positions in the school hierarchy, sitting up, adjusting our near-horizontal poses, or so much as opening our mouths to address the boy, was out of the question. We simply ignored him and waited.

My strongest recollection of that moment is the boy's face. He blinked incessantly while struggling to hold back tears. Suppressed panic is the only way to describe what I saw. His nostrils flared wide and sucked fresh oxygen in by the cubic litre. He had the jittery antelope posture I often saw in those who spent much of their time running away from others. His lips were caught in a wrestling match between a smile and a sob. It was a sad sight, the counterfeit cheer.

The terrified pupil had arrived for a scheduled shakedown. In exchange for the bag of goodies and fizzy drinks, the boy received 'protection', which meant he remained free from further harassment for the remainder of term. The food and drink he handed over were delicious. The ruffians found, as they always did, a new victim. School life went on. The expressions on the faces of the five village elders were variations of what I had seen on the junior student's face, back in school.

A Property and Population Inspection of a village this size should take two to three hours, at the most. However, a number of factors led us to remain longer than usual. There was the time of day: the afternoon approached its end, and no matter how swiftly we worked, it would be impossible to leave the hill before dark. Our best move was to complete the main phase of our business by early evening and remain in the village overnight (there were houses enough to accommodate the men). At dawn, we would complete the erasure, before heading off to rendezvous with 1st, 4th and 5th Companies. We radioed our intentions forward to the rest of the PPC. Another reason to stay was the village occupants' enthusiastic reception and the prepared toast. Here was an opportunity for a novel experience.

At the centre of the village was a large oval area, the major axis of which was aligned north-east to south-west. The houses were arranged in haphazard rows around the open ground. A network of vines stretched between the houses and supported a patchwork of brightly coloured sheets. These offered pleasant shade from the afternoon sun. Here and there, attached to the same vines, were humanoid effigies made from wood and straw. The dolls shared a single expression: serenity, by way of a smile. Bunches of fuchsia-coloured flowers were everywhere. Their placement appeared haphazard. Was this by design, or a by-product of haste and worry? The two rows of tables, while arranged less chaotically, could have done with some straightening. The same could be said for the chairs: on either side of the tables I counted at least seventeen unique styles of seating. I abandoned my counting endeavours when my head began to spin. Our photographers, on the other hand, were delighted. For those happy fellows, this village was an absolute bonanza.

The toast took place in the central oval, though not before a five-piece band and two singers delivered a fifteen-minute serenade. It was the most extraordinary music, and it took me back to many of our city's squares and parks where, in times past, Eastie minstrels often performed. Their music had a magnetic quality that held us in place while it danced in and out of our systems. The music played in this village was quite similar, and a good number of our men recognized and expressed their delight at these familiar sounds.

Given our numbers, it was impossible to seat all present. We selected a number of the men and asked them to join us at the tables, while the rest stood around the oval's periphery, together with the village occupants. Everyone received a drinking vessel (we must have used every cup, glass and mug in the village) and then we settled down. The five village elders, through the voice of their lyrical translator, made a toast to Our Dear Leader and to long and prosperous lives. The contents of my mug were peculiar, yet pleasant on the tongue. I could take a liking to this drink. Imagine a grapefruit, add a touch of smoke, a garnish of bitters, and you would have it. By the way, that potion was at least 70–80° proof, and with a kick to match.

With the toast done, we expected to set about our business. The village occupants, however, had other ideas: the following item on the agenda was a guided tour. Encouraged by the effects of the drink, and the fact there was no reason to make haste, I thought the tour an excellent idea. It would be helpful to our Recording and Documentation teams.

As we walked through the village, I noted the contradictions between how the messaging from above demanded we view Easties and what I saw, especially the architecture and infrastructure. We had been taught to perceive this nation and people as inferior to ourselves in every aspect, and it was true that a fair amount of what we destroyed in the East was in a neglected and run-down condition (proof of the wretched Eastie leadership). That said, the cracks, decay and faded paint could not hide the inherent beauty in much that we obliterated. I swatted away these inconsistencies by reminding myself of our mission for the Greater Glory.

There was nothing primitive about what we saw in the village. Almost all the Eastie-made objects were developed around mysterious compositions of circles, ovals and domes. All were constructed from wood, stone, grass, cloth in a manner that brought to mind the house at No. 17. The intricate forms were not all that amazed us. On five separate occasions I had engineers run up, panting as excited teenagers do, and express their appreciation and delight at the quality of construction achieved by the natives. I asked them to remain calm and carry on with their good work. Our continued surprise at the occupants' technical abilities was such that I even had a few of the men come up and ask whether we had stumbled into the remains of an ancient empire: they refused to accept everything around us was the work of the village occupants. I asked the men to look and think for themselves.

19

Our tour began with a trip to the well at the south-west end of the village, at the highest point of the hill. We learned that, according to stories passed down by the village occupants' ancestors, the well had constructed the hill to protect itself from the surrounding drought. Of course we knew this to be an unlikely tale, as there was a perfectly good geological justification for its existence. An explanation, I must admit, I did not know. Far more compelling than the tale of the well's origin was the irrigation network supplying water to the entire village, as well as to the crops and livestock lower down the hill. There was an interesting moment when I asked how the occupants processed the waste water for plant and animal use. They did not. I learned the water used for livestock consumption and crop irrigation was just as fresh as that drunk by the occupants. Their argument being, what they fed to the crops and animals, they fed to themselves. They were a truly fascinating people.

Our next destination was the largest building in the

village. Located at the opposite end of the oval to the well, it was an outstanding example of a well-crafted structure. The translator informed us the building was a ceremonial hall. Once every twenty-eight days, on the morning after a full moon, the entire village, together with some livestock, entered the space and thanked Nature for another moon cycle of life. The entrance was guarded by two immense wooden doors. Goodness knows what mechanical wizardry had been used to erect them (it was a puzzle our engineers were unable to solve). Their size was not all that impressed us: as they opened out to welcome in guests, the mighty doors turned on their hinges as if each weighed no more than a feather.

The interior snatched my breath away. The space was filled with light, though there was nothing inside that could truly be called a window. Cut into the top of the structure's dome was a series of twenty-one slits. Thin beams of sunlight shot in through the openings and bounced back and forth between the hundreds of mirrors that hung in the upper half of the space. The network of original and reflected sunbeams interacted with the dust particles inside and filled the interior with an otherworldly glow.

Six stone ventilation shafts, three on each side, were there to ensure adequate air circulation during ceremonies. The lower third of the interior walls was padded with a thick cushion of the same dried grass and fuchsia-coloured petals used by the occupants to welcome us to the village. The petals and grass were held in place with raffia netting. I silently applauded whoever had designed and erected such a structure.

The reaction of some of our cameramen to the building bordered on the unprofessional. Usually, such inability to control emotional expression would be met with a reprimand. However, their obvious excitement was an important factor in encouraging the villagers to let down their guard. Our sincere appreciation filled them with pride, a feeling I could relate to. Having such a magnificent building in one's community was indeed special. As we left the ceremonial hall and began the next stage of our tour, I sent a team downhill to ready our machinery, prepare two of our fuel trucks, and await further instructions.

Given the opportunity, the occupants would certainly have shown us the contents of every drawer, in every room, of every house in the village. Initially, I suspected all this to be no more than a delaying tactic. However, although I could not understand a word of what was said, the enthusiasm and pride they displayed suggested otherwise. Their lifestyle was based around various modular systems, each one dedicated to a specific function. For instance, all houses had equivalent ventilation systems. This simplified repair, because most of the village occupants understood how they worked and the standard design allowed for easy cannibalization of parts from old units. Given the waste in some of our own industries, I hoped our Recording and Documentation team's reports might work their way through the system and eventually inspire our national factory owners to think a bit harder, about the reuse of parts and materials.

The village occupants had modular systems for water, goats, crops, for everything. The system for selecting a house colour was also modular. While true, no two shades were alike, we learned they were all derived from combinations of a fixed set of colours mixed with a specific percentage of white. All colours were required to be present in the final shade, even if only a drop. This served as a reminder to the village occupants that they all came from the same source. I had never viewed our existence this way.

I found it quite touching, though not completely correct: their same was <u>not</u> our same.

Midway through the tour I was surprised by a gentle tug on my right index finger. Sticky and warm. I looked down and gazed into a pair of round, smiling eyes. The infant, perhaps driven by curiosity, had escaped her parent's clutches and come over for a closer look. She stood just below hip height and radiated an energetic joy that would have melted my heart, had a heart been present. As an officer of the PPC, I was obliged to maintain emotional distance and remind myself that young Easties grow into big Easties.

I allowed the infant to keep hold of my finger as we strolled through the village. She was happy to do so, and babbled away merrily. Occasionally, when in need of attention, she tugged at my trouser leg, and then tossed an excited stream of words at my ears. I nodded and made noises as if I understood her every word. The men had a laugh at my 'natural parenting' abilities. So did the village occupants, though their laughter did not come as easily as ours. The contrast in attitude between the self-confident infant holding onto my finger and her worried mother was as night is to day. The innocent fear nothing. The rest of us know better.

Well, all things come to an end. So did our visit. The Recording and Documentation teams let me know their work was done. It was time to 'complete' our inspection. Removing the infant's hand from my finger turned into a major struggle. Her protests began once she realized the walkabout was over. She gripped my finger as if holding on for dear life. I honestly worried about dislocation, or some other damage. Her strength and determination were surprising. She screeched and complained as the mother, assisted by two other village occupants, pried open her tiny fingers, and then led her away. The infant's teary eyes remained locked onto mine until they disappeared behind the wall of a nearby house. I did not see her again, though I still see her eyes from time to time: angry and disappointed. This war is an ugly business.

During our extensive tour of the village, a section of my mind had been absorbed with the search for a solution to a particular problem: how to encourage the occupants to assist or at least not kick up too much of a fuss during the final stages of our inspection. Were panic to break out, the topography of the hill with its thousand and one paths would have us chasing the occupants around for hours on end. I eventually based my plan on observations made in the ceremonial hall.

Our campaign in the East has taught me much about patterns of behaviour under particular circumstances, especially when the stakes are high. We are told East-ies lack the natural qualities expected in 'modern human beings'. So far, I am yet to discover any forms of behaviour in the Easties that I have not also seen exhibited by our own people. True, their customs and language are strange to my eyes and ears, but these are no more than accesso-ries. At their core, whether we like it or not, the Easties are mirror images of you and me. They too, when placed in life-or-death situations, become gullible souls. They find promise and hope in the tiniest gesture: in a smile, an act of politeness, in an empty promise. Desperation encour-ages most to believe there is a means to wish reality away and cancel the inevitable. The thinking behind my plan in the funny little village was based on this misapprehension.

The village occupants had by now become used to the sight of our recording teams going about their business. I asked the five village elders if they would be so kind as to arrange a mock ceremony. It would be for our cameras' benefit. At first, the elders appeared confused and said it was impossible to hold a ceremony, as it was neither morning nor the day after a full moon. I explained we did not wish for them to perform a <u>real</u> ceremony, rather an imitation. We had hoped to take a few extra photographs and some footage of them in ceremonial regalia before we left. I added that the sooner they prepared and posed for us, which we would appreciate deeply, the sooner we could be on our way. The idea of our departure lit fires of enthusiasm in the five village elders, and everyone else.

The village occupants dashed off to their houses and returned within half an hour, every one of them in their shiniest, ceremonial best. They looked magnificent. Spectacular! The sight was enough to make our photographers and camera crews very nearly lose their minds. One unfortunate soldier collapsed. I heard the medics sedated the man. Thankfully, he was back on his feet within hours.

The village occupants, together with numerous chickens and goats, took their positions inside the ceremonial hall. They began singing and chanting in a way that rang in my ears for weeks afterwards. The volume of their song drowned out the sound of everything outside, including the noise of our equipment making its way up the hill.

Midway through the mock ceremony, the last of our camera crews backed out of the hall. We then closed the mighty doors shut. The three bulldozers we had at our disposal were used to keep them that way. The occupants, on the inside, soon stopped their singing and began a noisy collective complaint, which over time, and up to a point, continued to increase in volume. The fuel trucks were moved into position. A team of agile men spent the next twenty-five minutes pouring kerosene into the six ventilation shafts. The occupants no longer complained. They screamed.

Evening approached. We sat at the tables on the village oval, which we arranged in three tidy rows. I issued the men extra rations of food and liquor, as well as commendations for their creative and efficient work. As we chatted, laughed, traded jokes and tales, the hall at the north-east end of the oval smouldered and crackled.

That night, when the fire in the ceremonial hall had become but a glow, we lay down to sleep on the beds, the furniture and on the floors of their houses. The sound of the wind, the night birds and the insects faded away, and for a quiet moment, there was nothing. The last I remember, before waking the next morning, was the black empty fog that descended upon me. There was no place for rest in that particular darkness.

In the morning, as we prepared to erase the village, the engineers arrived with an unusual request. Given the unconventional nature of the village buildings' construction, could I grant them permission to experiment with various demolition methods? I gave the teams an hour, and an order to leave the well alone. They turned the village to gravel within thirty-seven minutes.

Later, when our work was done and we prepared to leave, I noticed the framed portrait of Our Dear Leader lying on the ground. The explosion blasts had shattered the glass and twisted its frame. A splash of colour, revealed by the broken wood, caught my attention. I picked the frame up for a closer inspection. Those sneaky Easties . . . The photograph of Our Dear Leader had come from the front page of one of their newspapers. It was dated a month earlier, and had been folded to fit within the frame. The accompanying headline (translated by one of our men who was vaguely familiar with their language) compared Our Dear Leader to the Devil. The village occupants had placed it, for our benefit, over a colour group portrait of the Easties' leadership.

As we left the village I could not remove the image of Our Dear Leader from my mind. What made the photograph so discomforting to look at was the fact it clearly portrayed a man insane. With regard to our actions on that and many similar occasions . . . it was just another day at the office. This is the work that has finished me as a human being.

Yesterday I began to hear the village occupants' screams again. And worse, the screams and howls as I hear them today are not the sounds of beasts, but the cries of people like you and me, our sisters, mothers, fathers, sons, cousins, aunts, uncles, nieces, nephews, grandparents. These are who I destroyed. For the cause of the Greater Glory, in honour of Our Dear Leader, and in accordance with instructions, this sweet man, who spent sunny afternoons tickling your face with flowers, orchestrated the murder of every living creature in that funny little village.

I wish these memories formed part of a terrible dream

from which I could awake whenever the horror within becomes too much. Unfortunately, this is not the case. No magic in this world can extract me from the truth, or remove my spirit and replace it with a demon who I can accuse, blame and hold responsible for my choices. I was present all along: every day, every minute, every death.

As a child, I often tried to adjust the facts of a situation in order to get out of a bind. I was young and lacked the wisdom needed for such ploys to work. 'Let the truth be your friend,' Father would tell me. Today, while writing, I try and embrace truth as a friend, but tell me, what friend would bring such indescribable pain? The feeling I have is of a leaking heart, and what escapes is a bitter acid that consumes me again and again. I can do nothing. I feel myself becoming ever more hollow by the minute. It hurts, my love. And yes, I know this is the least I deserve. It still hurts that I can undo nothing.

~~Is it not sad~~

I hear detonations, four of them. I would say, going by their intensity, they landed approximately three kilometres south of our position.

My love, I could sit and share my sorrows with you for

another thousand hours. There is so much to say. However, at this late hour, I still have responsibilities. I need to attend to a few matters, and believe we still have some time before the enemy attacks. I shall return shortly, as soon as the situation permits.

20

It is hard to know what the enemy is up to. We waited an hour and a half for a sign, for movement. Nothing but heightened tension. We expected the four explosions to herald the start of their final assault, and our last battle. Instead they presented us with silence, and it is still quiet as I begin writing again.

Before the interruption, I was about to complain how now, when I need such a power most of all, I, Master of Erasure, am unable to wipe away the blood, death and destruction that stains my shadow. There is shame coming your way because of my work, and the only hope of avoiding it would be for the world to disappear in a flash. You will hear terrible stories about the activities of my brothers in arms and I: much worse than anything printed in the foreign news. Most of these tales will be true. During one of our last 'reasonable' exchanges with NDM High Command, we learned certain groups of our own people now ask uncomfortable questions regarding our wartime behaviour and methods. Our Dear Leader, quite naturally, was furious. The man truly believes himself and his actions to be above question. Apparently, due to these questions (and you will know more about this than those of us at the front), Our Dear Leader now alternates between calling the stories falsehoods conjured up by subversive elements, and declaring any who listen to be traitorous and mad. He has transformed National Radio, the NDM mouthpiece, into a laughing stock. If Our Dear Leader asked National Radio to claim that he single-handedly created the mountains, seas and all the lands on our planet, they would do so without hesitation. To you, and any others challenging this madness, I say: More speed!

Given time's current rate of evaporation, I feel a great pressure to write down as much as I can about my life in the PPC. This is my only worry: I scribble as fast as I can, yet have only scratched the surface of the truth of my work.

I beg you, do not waste your sympathy on me. If anything, feel sorrow for the ease with which I discovered and followed this path. Cry in anger at the encouragement and good wishes we received as we set off east, on our adventure for the Greater Glory. Tremble in horror at how one such as I can be so full of death and yet remain alive. Is that a life as it should be? As there is no understandable explanation for my actions, there can be no excuse. I chose to follow Our Dear Leader into this frenzy and now, with great embarrassment, I have a confession to make. When I strip away the bluster, the purposeless nationalism, what is left as a reason for me being here is my attraction to a smart uniform. That is it. No politics. No principles. Nothing more than fancy dress. What became of the man who was happy to live without direction? Where has that fellow gone? He was not there when I looked into the mirror this morning. That was someone else: a beast, a grand champion in the art of murder. I could not meet his eye.

A moment ago, one of the men called out: 'All right, sir? You have a funny look on your face.' I looked across the tent and held his gaze for a while. Will he be here tomorrow? Does he have a similar thought? I assured him all was fine. The man's eyes said he believed otherwise. It is always the eyes. The eyes say it all.

I must tell you, for the last three weeks I have seen eyes everywhere. I look at a bush and I see them. The leaves and shadows knit together and form pairs of eyes that look straight back at me. They read my thoughts. I feel them. I gaze at the clouds above, and in a matter of seconds I find myself staring back at someone up there who looks down on me. In the bark of a tree, the shadows across the floor, ripples in a nearby pool, on butterfly wings. Everywhere, I find eyes locking me into their gaze. They pierce my heart, they are in my head!

Most unnerving, though not unexpected, is the fact I know them all. I looked into every pair of those eyes as their bodies shut down and their souls left for other places. My relationship with their owners was always brief. Right up until their very last moment, they found the strength, courage, madness . . . to look out at the world, at me, with hope. I watched the eyes dart right and left as they urged Destiny to arrive and convince me to have a last-minute change of heart. I saw those eyes become cloudy with sad acceptance as it dawned on them . . . I was Destiny.

As I see them now, these eyes hold no bitter expressions, they have neither fury nor hunger for vengeance. All I can detect is a slight hint of pity and another expression that makes me shiver. Mother had the same look in her eyes when forgiving my mischief. I look at these eyes and understand my mind has broken. Why do I see them this way? Why do they look at me so? Why do they refuse to hate and despise me? There is no forgiveness for those engaged in my kind of business. Yet those eyes burn me with love, and I cannot escape them. What is their message?

I have a few ideas why the eyes have returned. During t

• • •

The long whistle of incoming guests. Shell after shell punctures the soil. There is no love in their actions. The guests announce themselves with earth-shaking thunder and bursts of explosive mutilation. Their greeting is as the fists of bloodthirsty gods, smashing into the ground again and again. They are here to deliver a reward. This is it! Murderous souls sigh their last, and bid farewell to this place en masse.

The bombardment ends, but silence does not fall. There is sobbing, wailing, moaning, screaming . . .

The shells, violent and merciless as they were, spared two of the tents. See them standing, quiet and lonely in the middle of slaughter's leftovers. One is untouched. Three diagonal gashes decorate the other.

*

A new thunder approaches. Much nearer to the ground, and closer by the second. There is shouting and cheering. The roar of righteous vengeance. There is blood in those cries. Leather boots, heavy soles smash and crush the grass. Makeshift paths are born. The breathing is heavy and fast and rough and wild. The ravenous warriors have but one simple task. If it lives, then it should not!

Hear the flash, crackle and spit of small-arms fire. Bullets escape and say 'Die!' as they pass through flesh and bone with minimal resistance. Today, Glory chooses to ride with the opposition.

In through the freshly sliced opening step five battle-frenzied soldiers. Eyes red and wild, and on the lookout for prey. There are men in the tent. Dead, and those about to die. The tent's contents, including the bodies, bear the brunt of the soldiers' fury: they are knocked, kicked about and treated with disdain.

Three of the men flip open jerrycan lids and pour the contents in every direction. Kerosene sloshes in abundance, and fumes fill the air.

*

A strip of sunlight cuts the tent in two. A corpse, face down on the floor, a fresh blood halo around the upper body. The soldier notices the makeshift table and chair built from wooden crates. The first drops of kerosene leave the can's mouth and splash onto one of the crates. The soldier stops. He looks. A frown ruffles his brows. His eyes, meanwhile, focus on an open journal. It looks lonely, and appears to be waiting. The soldier places the jerrycan on the floor next to the body, as a powerful curiosity urges him to take a closer look.

A black fountain pen rests in the gutter between the pages. The pages to the right of the pen are empty and ready to receive their share of what appears on the left: written in deep-blue ink, line after line of near perfect script. The soldier's eyes travel across the lines. A growing excitement fills his chest. It glows. During peaceful times, calligraphy had been his trade. It does not matter that the language of the journal is one he cannot understand. The form and precision of the handwriting sing out to him. Bloody soldier that he is, even this man does not believe all things deserve destruction. The pen and journal find a new home in his bag. The soldier then lifts the can from the floor and douses the table and chair and the bodies with kerosene. Happy cheers ring out as the tent and its contents begin to burn.

Time comes. Time goes.

A Glossary of
terms and abbreviations

NDM (National Defence Movement)

Came to power by way of military coup. Initially dedicated to dismantling corruption and boosting the nation's welfare. Having achieved their initial aims, and following the untimely loss of the Dear Leader, the NDM turned its attention to expansion and war.

The Greater Glory

A disastrous and megalomanic venture to conquer and ethnically cleanse the lands of the East. Driven by the ego and arrogance of Our Dear Leader. The circumstances of the author are a direct result of this venture.

Banality of Emotion

A concept burned into the minds of NDM officers. 'When engaged in duties deemed beneficial to the Greater Glory of the nation, situations may arise that necessitate taking radical action. To the casual observer, and the morally fragile, such actions may appear brutal and lacking in mercy.

During such moments, it is of vital importance that the officer of the National Defence Movement remains in control, and separates necessary action from the banality of emotion.'

Self-Identification
An essential indoctrination class in NDM officer training. It comprised chanting a number of carefully selected mantras for various lengths of time. The most important mantra had a sergeant demanding to know what the elite trainees were. They answered with a chorus of 'I am a God!' This would go on for many hours.

EDS (External Data and Security)
The division of the Ministry of Data and Security tasked with scooping up all available information regarding the goings-on in our neighbours' systems (political, economic, military, etc.) and translating this into useful intelligence.

DIDS (Division of Internal Data and Security)
The second division of the Ministry of Data and Security. Its remit was national observation, as there was a need to remain up to date on all comings, goings and sayings of

interest within the nation's borders. With particular attention paid to non-indigenous citizens.

DIE (Data and Information Extraction)
A section of the Division of Internal Data and Security tasked with processing and analysing the data collected by the various EDS and DIDS teams.

The National Registry
A cross-referential database of all citizens living within the nation's borders. This included: name, date of birth, place of residence, education, employment, family, friends, ethnicity, patterns of individual (and group) movement, consumption, literature, entertainment, health, leisure and politics.

Health For All
An extremely popular programme founded on the belief that a healthy society was a productive one, and that it was logical for the nation to take care of those who allowed it to function.

OEO (Office of Easterner Observation)

A department within the Division of Internal Data and Security whose sole function was to keep a watchful eye on the Easterner population living within the nation's borders.

Eastie

A derogatory term for Easterners (especially those resident within the nation) introduced to the nation by Our Dear Leader. The occasion being his response to an act of terror. Originally used by the OEO as an abbreviation for 'Easterners' but overheard and transformed into an insult by the NDM Messaging and Public Relations team.

PDE (Potentially Disruptive Eastie)

A category of Eastie identified by the OEO (through analysis of collated data) as likely to become involved in, or support, activities against the national interest.

The Oath

An obligatory oath (to the nation and Our Dear Leader) to be taken by all Easties resident within the nation's borders. Its primary function was to identify Potentially Disruptive Easties (PDEs), who were then placed on the Action

Pending Register. Residency permits were provided to all Easties who took the Oath.

APR (Action Pending Register)

A database of Easties managed by the NDM Ministry of Housing and Justice (MHJ), in conjunction with DIDS. As the relationship with the East deteriorated, retaliatory sanctions were taken against resident Easties. The groups and individuals listed for targeting were selected from the APR. Easties listed in the APR were not given access to residency permits.

UR (Unlawful Resident) Status

Easties without residency permits were given 'Unlawful Resident' (UR) status.

DI (Declaration of Illegality)

A pronouncement given by the MHJ to any Eastie with Unlawful Resident (UR) status. The sanctions for a DI included immediate forfeiture of all property (and items unable to be carried without assistance), as well as deport-ation to the land of ancestral origin.

PIO (Property Integrity Office)

An enclave of the Division of Internal Data and Security within the Ministry of Housing and Justice. The PIO managed all state properties through various Site Inspection Units, which handled all on-the-ground activities.

SIU (Site Inspection Unit)

These units were paramilitary teams, each with an area of specialization, for example the preparation of properties for renovation. In such cases, preparation commenced with the extraction of all occupants with UR status. The properties selected for preparation were always associated with Easties listed in the APR.

AO (Appropriation Order)

An official document from the MHJ that permitted the relevant SIU to begin immediate preparations.

Unlawful Resident Transfer Squad

Worked in partnership with an SIU. They facilitated the transport of evicted Easties to the appropriate departure points.

PI (Process Inspector)
Trained individuals tasked with monitoring SIU activities. Occasionally gaps appeared between theory and practice. The PI prescribed solutions for areas in need of improvement.

Situational Attitude
A training method created to improve the operations of SIU commanders. It taught how best to express the three Ds: Disdain, Disgust and Disinterest.

Erasure
A concept developed by Our Dear Leader, during his time as head of the Ministry of Data and Security's Office of Strategic Possibilities. He believed the complete erasure of such elements as language, traditions, music, art and industry would, over time, allow for a people to disappear from history.

PPC (Property and Population Control Battalion)
Nicknamed 'The Factory Boys' because of their mobile processing units. They were an effective part of Our Dear Leader's erasure machine. Their remit included the

'preparation of land for further civilization through the removal of unnecessary artefacts'. This was done by way of Property and Population Inspections.

PPI (Property and Population Inspection)

The recording followed by total destruction of any object, no matter the size, that could bring joy or hope to the hearts of Easties. The PPC translated Our Dear Leader's wishes into actions.